More Than Enough

Also by John Fulton

Retribution

More Than Enough

JOHN FULTON

WILLIAM HEINEMANN : LONDON

More Than Enough

He was stretching and still looking at the sky. 'It's fresh out here,' he said, 'not cold. It feels good.' My father liked to feel good about almost everything, and he liked other people to feel good about things, too. People create life for themselves, and so they might as well create a good one. That was more or less the way he thought.

Inside, I was happy to see my father's papers scattered over the kitchen table – more proof of his studying – which would be important for my mother to see when she returned from ZCMI, where she sold cosmetics during the day. My father's latest ambition, and the reason we had moved from Boise to Salt Lake, was to become a certified public accountant after a two-year program at Salt Lake Community College. It was important that he do well because his courses were expensive and because the last year in Boise – where he'd been let go from National Harvester, and from Raider Truck Company before that – had been difficult for us. But he was not always, I knew even then, the most disciplined of students. Once I had looked at a sheet of his work left out on the counter and saw that, for the most part, his answers were wrong. I was a good student, especially at math, and was getting A's on my Algebra II tests in my first semester as a sophomore at Billmore High. I could see what he had done wrong, the mistakes he was making. But I didn't mention it to him, and I decided not to look at his work again. I was sure he'd improve, fall into the swing of being a student. Besides, he was doing his part, working twenty hours a week at a garage downtown, and was often tired and a little moody.

After studying for a while, Jenny and I went out to our ten-by-ten square of backyard and untangled Noir from his chain. He put on his usual show of unrestrained happiness — leaping, barking, pouncing at our legs — because he'd been freed from his cramped little space and knew he was going for a walk. It was great to see and tended to infect me with the same ridiculous excitement, even if I'd had a terrible day. Noir was a funny name for my dog because he was large and entirely white save for the smallest streak of black on one leg. He'd been named by a German hippie, who had lived two apartment doors down from us in Boise and had given him to me soon before we left for Salt Lake. I hadn't much liked the name at first, though later it seemed to work; it simply became him, whether he was white or not.

With Noir running in front of us, we headed up Ensign Down Boulevard, the main street that ran through the Downs. Like many neighborhoods in Salt Lake, the Downs was built over the foothills in a town where money and class were easy to see: those who had them lived up high against the mountains closer to their God, and those who didn't lived down low, farther away from someone else's God. The streets on the bottom half of the Downs were numbered. We lived in a duplex on Second Street, where most of the small two-room houses were rented by medical students, single mothers, and bachelors who lived with other bachelors. A mile or so up Ensign

Down Boulevard, large new houses with balconies, sloping yards, and huge windows had been built into the hills on streets that had names like Joy Road, Paradise Drive, Marvel Circle. Above these neighborhoods, bulldozers carved the land into roads and partitioned it into lots, where dozens of new houses were just then being constructed. It was the early nineties, and there was a housing boom in Salt Lake and in the rest of the country, too. You read about it in the papers and heard about it on the news. People were making money, inflation was low and under control, and though I did not know exactly what that meant, I knew it was a good thing. I knew our family had reason to hope for the best.

Jenny and I were headed to the neighborhood of half-built houses and muddy streets and yards, where NO TRESPASSING signs warned walkers-by to stay out of the construction sites. Because most of those houses had no walls yet, you could walk through the frames and into the middle of the structure, look up at the sky, and imagine the height of the absent ceilings, the color of the carpet not yet laid, the number of rooms and windows, bathrooms, balconies, and porches. A few houses were closer to completion, and once Jenny and I had gotten into one of them. It was a three-story house off to the side of a road so freshly asphalted that you could still smell the tar in the air. Inside, large stacks of white tile lay covered in plastic. Written in pencil on the blank white walls were words like SINK, BATHTUB, KITCHEN COUNTER, WASHER AND DRYER, WOOD-BURNING STOVE. These objects lay heavily over the floor, wrapped in plastic and brown paper, waiting to be installed. They amazed Jenny and me, and we ripped a hole in the covering of the largest object and felt the cold enamel of a tub.

As sometimes happened on our walks, we were followed by a pack of neighborhood boys, some from my class at Billmore, and other, smaller boys who tagged along. They lived in the large, silent houses far above our duplex and knew that we were strangers who lived in every way below them. As we climbed higher into those wealthy neighborhoods, more and more of them came out of their houses and walked behind us. In the past, they hadn't done much to us. They'd called us names. They'd thrown a rock or two. But mostly they'd kept their distance and let us be.

That afternoon they stopped leaving us alone. It was a gray day in early January, and you could see the storm trapped up in the mountains and guess, as my father had, that it would soon be snowing down in the valley. A car or two drove up the hill, but it was around four o'clock, which meant the street was mostly deserted and we could easily walk up the middle of it and let Noir roam free, searching the wet yellow lawns for places to pee. At our backs lay the city – the State Capitol, the LDS Mormon Office Tower, Temple Square, Main and State Streets, the Avenues, and the Upper Benches running south along the Wasatch Front, where Big and Little Cotton Wood Canyons led up to the ski resorts. From the top of the Downs, you could easily see the endless grid of streets stretching west beneath a haze of pollution. When we neared the end of Ensign Down Boulevard, where the asphalt gave way to gravel, and then mud, and from where we could see the strange neighborhood of skeletal houses, Jenny looped her arm in mine. The boys had come within a few paces of us, so close that we could hear the crisp slap of the baseball that they threw back and forth across the street. 'Should we run?' Jenny whispered.

'No,' I said, angry that my sister failed to see that running was not an option for me. The baseball shot overhead and was caught by a kid who'd sprinted out in front of us. He threw it back just above our heads, so close that I flinched, and Jenny looked away and let out a shriek. 'Shush,' I said beneath my breath. I was embarrassed to be seen with my sister, who was fourteen, eighteen months younger than me. We'd both begun irritating each other during our first months in Salt Lake. But I had no friends yet, no one else to spend time with, and neither did she. Another kid ran out in front of us, where he caught the ball and hurled it – again just over our heads – to a boy who stood behind us. Jenny wanted to stop, but I pressed forward – boys on all sides of us now – until we were walking over the mud of an unnamed street on the sides of which construction vehicles – a small yellow bulldozer covered in dirty snow and two pickup trucks that said ZION CONTRACTORS on the sides of them – had been parked. Building materials – boards, bricks, coils of black hose, and lead pipe – lay stacked and partially covered beneath canvases held down by large rocks. Noir ran between the boys, wagging his tail and being too damn friendly. He leapt at them, his tongue dangling. When one of the smaller kids took a kick at him, he thought they were playing and began turning circles; then he lunged through the mud and into the middle of one of those large stick houses. The boys were dressed more or less alike in yellow and orange ski parkas from which dangled square paper passes from Alta or Snowbird or whatever expensive resort their families had last skied at. They wore bulky sports shoes of all colors – blue, black, red – with thick rubber heels that had little transparent plastic windows in them. Those were expensive shoes, I knew – eighty-dollar shoes. The kids were blond, their hair cut so short that it grazed their golden scalps. They looked less like a religion than like a race, a kind of people. That wasn't a nice thought, but it was how I felt about them then.

'Hey,' one of them said, 'your dog's pissing on that house.'

Noir was in somebody's future living room or kitchen lifting his leg on a two-by-four. 'Noir,' I called out. He glanced at me quickly, put his leg down, and began sniffing the cement foundation for his next place to pee.

'What did you call him?' one of those kids asked.

Jenny and I stopped walking; I turned around and tried to address whoever had said that, but they were like the same kid in different sizes. 'Noir,' I said.

'Moir,' the kid with the baseball in his hand said. He threw it, again over our heads. 'What's Moir?' My dog looked our way, confused by hearing his name tossed around like that. But he soon went back to his animal chores, sniffing and searching out that house for whatever he could find.

'Noir.' I spelled it out. *'N-o-i-r.'*

'That means 'black' in French,' one of them said. 'He's white. Why did you call him black when he's white?'

That question bothered me, since his name made no sense to me, either. 'Maybe I wanted to call him what he's not,' I said.

'He shouldn't be peeing on these houses,' a kid said. He was one of the few kids who had something different about him. He wore glasses and had a chubby face. He bent down then, grabbed some dirty snow, and began to pack it. The two smaller kids on either side of him did the same, after which the kids on all sides of us started packing muddy snow into hard, brown balls. I felt Jenny moving in still closer and holding on tighter. She wanted to walk down the hill and in the direction of our house. But I didn't think we should look like we were retreating. So instead we followed Noir into the half-built house – a cement foundation and stick frame – where he'd been peeing. We walked over the driveway and through what must have been the garage and into the kitchen or the family room. Had Jenny and I been there alone, we might have surveyed the place and begun claiming rooms for ourselves, which we'd often done. 'This is my room and this is my bathroom,' we'd say, running from room to room until the whole house had been claimed and divided between us.

'Hey,' a kid said from behind us, 'it says no trespassing.' I heard someone kick the sign that had been stuck out front in the mud. The pack of kids followed us into the house anyway. We could see them through the walls of two-by-fours in front of us and to the sides of us, dirty snowballs in their gloved hands. 'Can't you read?' the same voice asked.

Someone threw a snowball that hit my sister in the back. 'Ouch,' she said. I could tell she wanted to run. But I squeezed her hand tightly to let her know that she couldn't show fear.

'Sure,' I said then, turning around and facing the chubby kid with glasses. He was the one talking. 'We can read.' I looked around for Noir, who had disappeared. I wanted him close by. I thought he might seem threatening, though I knew he wouldn't hurt anyone.

'Then why are you trespassing?'

'You're trespassing, too,' I said.

'That's not what I asked you.' He threw the baseball again, this time so close to my head that I had to dodge it.

'Don't do that,' I told him. Someone behind me threw a snowball that hit my side. I didn't budge despite the fact that it stung like hell.

'What're your names?' the kid with the glasses asked.

I told him.

'You don't go to the ward,' he said.

'No.'

'What ward do you go to?' some kid behind us asked. Jenny wanted to turn around, but I didn't let her.

'Tell them to stop throwing snowballs,' she said to me. Another came flying at us then, though we dodged it. 'Stop throwing snowballs!' she shouted at them.

'Shush,' I said.

'What ward do you go to?' the kid with the glasses asked again.

'None,' I said.

One of the smaller kids had picked up a board from the ground and was smacking it against something.

'What do you believe, then?' he asked.

'Nothing.' I took my glasses off and zipped them into my coat. They were unattractive and had thick black frames. But I knew that we could not afford to replace them. Things went a little blurry, and I had to squint at the kid to keep his features in focus.

'How can you believe nothing?'

'We're Catholic,' Jenny said.

'No we're not,' I said, not sure why my sister would tell this lie.

'We go to the Catholic church,' she said.

'We don't,' I said. 'We don't believe in God.'

The kid with the fat face was tossing the baseball up and down in one hand. 'You are,' he said. 'You're Catholic. You believe in the pope.'

'No,' I said. 'We aren't. We don't.' The fact that we believed in nothing, no God, no pope, nothing, had just become important to me. It was the only thing that I could own at that moment.

'You're lying,' he said.

Two more snowballs hit me – one in the side and one in the back of the head. Jenny ducked down and held her hands out. I bent down and picked up a board. There were boards and discarded nails all over the cement floor. The kids around us also picked up boards, though not the one who was talking. He was still tossing the baseball up and down in his hand.

'Don't do that,' Jenny said, looking at me and the other kids. She wanted us to put the boards down. I saw Noir sprinting toward us along the muddy road, happy in that stupid, excessive way of dogs.

'You're lying,' the kid with the glasses said again. Then, without blinking, he hurled the ball into my gut. For an instant, bent over and wheezing, I went blind. The board dropped from my hand.

'Catholic shit,' one kid said.

'Steven,' my sister said, though I no longer knew where she was. I felt the ice-cold concrete beneath my hands and knew that I was on my knees. Noir yelped with pain and then began to bark. I opened my eyes, reached for the baseball, and hurled it at the fat-faced kid, missing him. Something hit me from behind and I went down, tasting blood, warm and sudden, on my lips. Two or three drops hit a patch of snow in front of me, and I heard Jenny scream. The fat kid was straddling me, his knees pressing into my back. He put his hand on the top of my head, took a fist of my hair, and pulled until I felt a clump come lose. I screamed and he pushed my cheek into the concrete until I was silent again. In front of me, I saw multiple pairs of new, expensive sports shoes walking over the ground. 'Beg for mercy,' the kid on top of me said. He turned my head and pushed my other cheek into the concrete.

'It's cold,' I said.

'Mercy,' he said. 'Say it.'

'Mercy,' I said. But he didn't stop whatever terrible thing he was doing to me with his knee.

'Your sister ran home,' some other kid said.

'Louder,' the kid on top of me said. 'Say, "I beg for mercy".'

'Fuck you.'

'You're making me do this.' He cocked my arm behind my back and slowly pushed it up toward my shoulder. 'Say it,' he said, cranking my arm up another notch. I yelped and tried to ask for mercy, though no words came out. Tears streaked down my face. 'He's crying,' some kid said.

'I'm not,' I managed to say.

'You will be soon.' The fat kid repositioned his knee, stood up a little on his other leg, and fell on me with all his weight. 'One more time,' he said. But instead of falling on me again, he grabbed my arm and slowly, with what must have been all his strength, lifted my bent arm, elbow first, upward over the back of my head until my shoulder quivered with pain from a place deep inside the socket where I'd never felt pain before. 'Say it,' he said fiercely into my ear. I felt the muscle begin to tear, slowly, then more quickly. 'Jesus,' someone said. I heard a distinct pop of bones and then my own voice screaming, long and sharp. My arm went slack and my chest collapsed. 'Oh,' he said, standing up.

'What did you do to him?' another kid asked. I rolled over and saw the weird frame of the house above me seeming to lean into the air and hover there, bend and quiver the way something reflected on water might. The fat face of the kid who had hurt me floated into this picture. His stupid open eyes told me that he was afraid before he turned and ran off with the other kids.

Lying on the concrete foundation, I felt waves of pain roll over me and cold air move through my throat and into my lungs. Noir whimpered above me and licked my face. 'No,' I said. Speaking hurt. Half of me was abuzz with hot pain. I struggled to my knees, pushing myself up with the arm that seemed to work. My other arm was bent in a strange way so that the palm of my hand pointed away from me. I tried not to look at it. Looking at it made it hurt more. The first steps were nearly unbearable. When I concentrated and breathed and walked slowly, the pain eased a little. Whimpering, Noir walked at my side. 'No. No,' I said for some reason. I heard a car rush by, and then another. The air was gray and I thought maybe it was snowing lightly, though I only half registered this fact. At one point, I looked around and knew from the cars and houses that I had gone too far down the hill and had passed our duplex. Finally, at my front door, I could not work the key into the lock, and so, like a stranger, I rang the doorbell.

'Steven,' my father said. Usually when I arrived home, my father would not lift his face from his math textbook to look at me. He often tried to seem busy with his schoolwork when my mother and I were at home. That afternoon, he dropped his notepad on the entryway table and let me in. 'Jesus Christ,' he said. 'What happened to you?' He touched my shoulder and I screamed. 'Oh, God,' my father said. 'I'm sorry. I didn't mean to do that.'

'I got lost,' I said. 'I didn't know where I was.'

My mother was running for the phone. 'I'm calling an ambulance.'

'We can't call an ambulance,' my father said. 'We can't afford a bill like that.'

'Look at him, for God's sake,' my mother said. She held the phone in her hand but wasn't dialing. They were both looking at me now.

'We'll drive him ourselves,' my father said.

'How did this happen?' my mother asked me. She came at me with a washcloth she'd just run under the water. 'Stand up straight,' she said. 'Stand up so that I can take care of this cut.'

'I can't,' I said, trying to stand straight. 'It hurts too much.'

'Jesus.' I saw the fear in her face. She bent down and wiped at my mouth. Her perfume was almost acidic and turned my stomach. Because she had to wear the scents she sold at work, she often smelled harsh and floral.

'Ouch!' I yelled. The blood on the cloth scared me. I hadn't thought I was bleeding that much.

'Your arm,' she said, 'what happened to your arm? What happened to his arm?'

My father bent down, gently lifted my red parka, and looked inside. 'I think he's dislocated his shoulder,' he said.

'It was an accident,' I said, knowing I could not become a snitch. 'I fell.'

'Who did this to you, Steven?' my mother asked. 'Your sister already told us you were having an argument with someone. Who were you arguing with?'

'No one did anything to me,' I said. 'Where's Jenny? What happened to Jenny?'

'Let's get him in the car,' my father said.

'I want to come,' Jenny said. She was crying and curled up in the fat green TV chair that we had bought from Deseret Industries and that smelled faintly of cat piss, so faintly that we had all decided to believe it wasn't cat piss and never mentioned it to one another.

I yelped. My father had touched my injured arm again. 'I'm sorry,' he said. He was trying to stand me up and turn me toward the door.

'Let me walk myself,' I yelled, even though talking hurt. Each word seemed to push against a tightness in my chest. There were two spots of blood on my white tennis shoes. 'Am I bleeding a lot?'

'Not a whole lot,' my father said.

'He is,' my mother said. 'Look at him. Somebody did that to him.'

'You're not helping,' I heard my father whisper to her.

He looked at me. 'It's just your lip. It looks like you cut your lip a little.'

We were outside now. The air was gray and the snow had begun falling in heavy sideways sheets. My parents walked on both sides of me, their arms out to catch me if I fell. 'It hurts to talk,' I said.

'It hurts him to talk,' Jenny said, her voice panicky.

'I'm not injured too badly, am I?' I had to whisper. If I whispered, the pain wasn't as bad.

'No,' my father said. 'No, you're not.'

I didn't remember getting in the car. I remember only opening my eyes and seeing that I was in the backseat with Jenny's hand in my good hand. 'I'm sorry for running,' she whispered.

'Running from what?' my mother asked. My father was outside brushing a thin dust of snow away from the windows. 'You tell me what happened,' she said. I squeezed Jenny's hand as tightly as I could to let her know that she'd better not say anything, and she didn't. When my father sat down in the car, my mother looked at him and said, 'He needs an ambulance, Billy. We need to call an ambulance.'

'He's fine,' my father said.

'He is not fine,' she said.

'You're scaring him,' he said. Then he whispered in her ear. 'He might be in shock. The best thing to do is to keep him talking.'

'I hate this,' my mother said.

'I can hear you,' I said. It hurt less to talk now that I was sitting and speaking in a very soft voice. 'I'm not in shock.'

'Good,' my father said. 'That's what we want to hear.' He was driving now and trying to look at me in the rearview mirror while he kept an eye on the road. 'I want you to keep talking to me. I want you to tell me how you are. How are you?'

'Okay, I guess.' If I concentrated, I could keep the pain at a distance, like a sound you hear at night in your bed that grows farther and farther away. When I looked down at my injured arm, it didn't seem to be my arm. It felt unnaturally attached to me, awkward and foreign.

'He's staring at his arm,' Jenny said to my parents.

'Look at me,' my father said, by which he meant that I should address him in the rearview mirror. I did. 'Good boy. Now speak to me, Steven. Tell me something. Anything.'

'Where's Noir?' I asked. I couldn't remember at that point whether he had followed me home or not. I remembered only hearing him yelp soon after I had hit the concrete.

'He's fine. He's back home. What else would you like to talk about?'

'Could we talk about our house?' I asked. 'Could we talk about moving up the hill?'

'Of course we could,' he said. In fact, the house was one of his favorite topics of conversation.

'When are we moving up the hill?' Jenny asked.

'Soon,' he said. 'The times are pretty good just now.

There's a lot of activity going on, and we'll be able to take advantage of that. As soon as I'm a certified accountant, we should make our move. No more than a year, a year and a half maybe.'

'Please,' my mother said, 'let's not go through this. Steven is hurt, for God's sake.'

'We're not going through anything,' my father said.

'No more about the house,' she said.

'It will have three stories, right?' I asked. My father nodded. 'It will be up on Green Hill or Lemon Circle?' I asked, referring to two of the nicest streets above our duplex, streets where the kids who had hurt me that day probably lived.

'Sure,' my father said. 'Those are both possibilities. Or we'll take one of the new ones they're building now. Those look promising.'

'And it will have a trampoline and swimming pool in the backyard?' Jenny added.

'No,' my father said, surprising me because we had always planned to have a swimming pool and trampoline and because I had assumed that great plans – at least in the realm of dream – never had to change. 'The trampoline can stay. But the swimming pool is inside the house now . . . just off the living room. What's the use of an outside pool in a place where it snows five months of the year?' He gestured to the world outside our car, where the snowfall had become so thick that you could barely see the ghostly outlines of the mountains in the distance. 'It will be enclosed and climate-controlled so that you kids can swim in the middle of a blizzard if you want. We'll be able to enter it from the living room or kitchen through sliding glass doors. A deck will lead from the pool out onto the backyard where you can sun yourselves in the summer or just sit and drink Cokes and listen to music with friends.'

I looked over at Jenny, who was smiling and who clearly liked the sound of the new pool as much as I did. 'My room,' she said (and I knew very well what she was about to demand since she had done so many times before), 'will have two large windows and will be far away from Steven's, all the way down the hall from his, and right across the hall from a bathroom.' Then she said, 'My bathroom.' I usually snapped back at her for her nasty possessiveness and her desire to escape me, but Jenny and I had been in cramped quarters for as long as we could remember, and that afternoon I understood her wish for her own space, for two windows and a bathroom all her own. I wanted that, too.

'Of course,' my father said to Jenny. 'You will have your own bathroom. Steven will have one, too. I will have one and your mother will have one. And,' he added, 'we will also have a guest bathroom. Five bathrooms.' He lifted his hand from the steering wheel and put out five fingers, wiggling them a little for emphasis. I imagined these bathrooms, my mother's done in pink colors with little pink seashell soaps beside the sink, Jenny's done in purple with seashell soaps of that same color, my father's bathroom and my bathroom in marine blue or in rustic earth colors, though I didn't know much about how bathrooms should look. I knew only that there would soon be five bathrooms where there was now only the hurried and shameful privacy of one.

'How are you feeling, Steven?' My mother had turned around and I could see from her face – tired and worried – that she didn't believe a word my father had said and that she was in no mood to pretend that she did.

'Fine,' I said. 'Great.'

'Great,' she said, laughing a little. 'How could you feel great?'

'I just do,' I said.

My mother said something odd then. 'You don't have to feel great for our sakes, you know. You're allowed to feel however you feel.'

I didn't understand her and neither did my father. 'Why are you telling him that?' he asked. 'He's doing just fine and you're telling him he shouldn't be.'

'He's hurt, Billy,' my mother said, 'and we're acting like nothing has happened.'

'We're not acting like anything,' my father said. 'We're just making conversation.'

'We're talking nonsense. We're talking about bathrooms we don't even have.'

'I like to talk about them,' I said. 'It makes me feel better to talk about them.' My parents were too angry to continue speaking, and whatever spell I had been under, whatever state of mind had kept the pain away, was broken now. I looked down at my lap and saw again how my palm and forearm were turned up at a wrong angle. My upper arm was swollen, and I moved the ice bag that – though I didn't remember it – my father must have given me farther up on my shoulder. I felt a stabbing pang, then another and another. 'Jesus,' I said, trying to concentrate and keep the pain away.

'We're almost there, kiddo,' my mother said.

'A minute ago,' my father said, 'he was just fine. And now, no thanks to you, dear, he's in agony.

'Please,' I said, 'please don't argue.'

They were quiet for a while, and I was glad since the pain now demanded all my concentration and made the tears come to my eyes, though I managed not to sob or make any humiliating childish noises. I just let the tears fall and held on to my arm and was thankful for the silence until my mother turned around again and said, 'Please, Steven, tell us how this happened. We know you didn't fall. Who did this to you?'

'I fell,' I said. 'It was an accident.'

'Jenny,' my mother said, 'what happened to your brother?' I looked at my sister and tried to tell her with my eyes, full of tears or not, that if she said anything I would hurt her, I would make her life miserable.

'I don't know exactly,' she said, looking down in her lap.

'Jenny,' my mother said.

Jenny looked up. 'Why don't we believe in God?' she asked.

There was a silence in the car. 'Because we would

rather not believe something just to make ourselves feel better about the world,' my father said. 'Because we're not afraid of the truth. Because what we have is what we see in front of us, and that's good enough.' We had heard our father's lectures on this subject before whenever we asked this question. He had always felt strongly about his atheism. He seemed to feel that he – and his family – were stronger because of it.

My mother turned around and looked at Jenny. 'Why are you asking?'

'Because that's what the boys who hurt Steven wanted to know.'

'Shut up!' I yelled, even though my lungs felt as if they would shatter. 'Shut the fuck up.' I wanted to kick her, but I didn't have the strength.

'They were Mormons,' my sister continued, having decided to betray me completely. 'Kids from our neighborhood. Kids who live up the hill.'

'Shut up!' I was crying out loud now and hated her for reducing me to sobs.

'Did you hear that, Billy?' my mother said. 'The Mormon kids. Those little brats. When we're done at the hospital, I'm going to find them. I'm going to go to their houses.'

'No, you're not,' I said.

'Damned if I'm not. Look at what they did to you.'

'Please don't,' I said. I looked up at the rearview mirror where I met my father's eyes and thought I saw that he understood me, that he knew that his son could not become a snitch.

'No one's going over to anyone's houses,' he said. 'Let's just get to the hospital. We'll think about the rest later.'

My mother turned back around in her seat. 'We'll see,' she said under her breath. I knew then that my father would do what he could for me. We were all quiet again, and I hoped it would stay that way until we arrived at the hospital, though finally Jenny sighed. 'I wish we went to church like everybody else in this city. I wish we believed in God.' She was writing her initials over and over again in the steamed glass of her window.

'We believe in ourselves, Jen,' my father said enthusiastically. 'We're not afraid of the fact that we have no one and nothing else to rely on. People don't get anywhere thinking that something out there is going to make life better. You think that way' – he cleared his throat – 'and you never have to look at yourself and see who's really running your life.'

Jenny didn't answer him. None of us did except for my mother, who laughed bitterly at his remark.

'I'm not joking, Mary,' he said. I could tell by the way he leaned into the steering wheel that he was irritated and maybe even hurt. 'Please stop writing on the window, Jenny,' he said. 'That makes a mess. And who do you think has to clean it up?'

'Okay,' she said, and stopped.

The hospital was called The Richmond Clinics, a huge, newly constructed building with white siding and hundreds of large windows that emanated a bronze light in the dark snowfall. 'Don't let him slip,' my mother said as we walked through the snow-covered parking lot. I could stand up straighter now, though I found that hunching over reduced the pain and made breathing easier. The blood on my face had dried, and my lips and cheeks felt stiff and swollen. A series of black glass doors that read EMERGENCY slid open for us, and signs for check-in led into a brightly lit waiting room with rows of padded chairs and tables, where a few old people sat quietly reading. There were almost no signs of other people's emergencies except for a small boy who sat beside his parents holding a white compress stained with blood to his head. 'What's wrong with you?' he asked my sister when we sat down across from him.

'I'm just fine,' Jenny said. She took off her puffy winter coat, which she did right away whenever she entered a place because she hated to appear fat. She wore a pink sweater and white Levi's, clothes that looked new and expensive despite the fact that my mother had bought them secondhand. For some reason, clothes always looked new when Jenny wore them. She was a pretty girl with long curly hair that reached the small of her back. She made sure a strand or two hung down the side of her face, aware that this gave her what she called 'girl appeal', which meant something like sex appeal, though as a fourteen-year-old freshman in high school, she hadn't yet developed. She was still too flat to need bras and didn't have much shape in her hips. All the same, she acted like an adolescent girl, sealing herself away for hours in the bathroom, arguing with my mother about how a young girl should wear her hair, and reading women's magazines, one of which she picked up now and opened while she talked to the boy across from her.

'They're going to have to use a needle,' the kid said. 'I need stitches and I might have a concussion.'

'Ouch,' Jenny said, though she didn't of course really feel his pain. She'd just said that to be a charming, conversational girl, which she often tried to be. On the front of her magazine, a woman looked out at us, her eyes blue and hungry, and her hair flung back and wind tossed. 'My brother's hurt, too. He did something to his shoulder. He dislocated it, we think.' TWENTY TIPS FOR GIRLS WITH THIN LIPS, the front of her magazine said. I understood then why the woman on the cover was pursing her red, glossy mouth into a whistle; she was showing the world how full her lips were, how full a woman's lips should be. The kid asked what dislocating a shoulder meant and Jenny did something fancy with her fingers and made a popping sound with her mouth to illustrate the idea. 'It's when your arm gets pulled out of joint.'

The little kid looked at me, his eyes swollen from tears, and I think he saw in my face exactly what I saw in his: the fear of what had happened to us and the fear of what would soon happen – the needles, the stitches, the doctors and nurses using incomprehensible words. I also knew that Jenny, unhurt and determined to be pleasant and social while also fingering through her magazine, did not understand the first thing about our fear, and I wished that she were hurt, too, cut or stung or poisoned or anything that would keep her from saying the terribly kind and untrue thing she said next. 'You'll be okay, I'm sure. You won't even remember it happened to you tomorrow.'

A man came into the room and called the kid's name, which made him panic. He dropped his bloody bandage and flailed his arms when his father picked him up and said, 'No! I won't go! I won't!' though he was easily carried beyond the flapping double doors, and I listened for his voice until I could no longer hear it. The same man returned and called my mother and father and me to a desk where he gave my father a clipboard of paperwork and a pen with the name of the hospital – THE RICH-MOND CLINIC – written on it, which for some reason made me feel better about the place.

'We're not sure what happened to him,' my mother said. 'He can't stand up straight. It hurts him to talk too much.'

The man's name tag said NURSE DOUGLAS. He was large and wore a beard and had powerful-looking arms – not my idea of a nurse. He looked inside my parka and, without hesitation, said, 'That's a dislocated shoulder. He should be able to stand up again as soon as his muscles start relaxing.'

'He's in terrible pain,' my mother said. 'Could you give him something now? A pill? Anything for the pain?'

'We can't give him anything until he's checked in. As soon as we can, we'll take care of him. He'll have the best doctor in the state.' I believed him when he had said they'd take care of me, and I was ready to surrender myself into his hands. My mother squeezed my good hand in hers and I knew that she had calmed down, that she believed things would turn out for us. 'So how did this happen, Steven?' Nurse Douglas asked.

'I fell,' I said. 'I was playing football.'

To my surprise, my mother let this go while Nurse Douglas made some notes and started typing on the computer in front of him. 'Football,' he said, 'that's a rough sport. We see a lot of young football players in here.' He looked up from his computer screen then and studied the plastic insurance card my father had given him only minutes ago. 'I hope we don't have a problem, Mr. Parker,' the nurse said.

'How so?' my father said. I felt my mother's hand stiffen again.

'My computer is not showing that you're covered.'

'Of course we're covered,' my father said. For some reason, my father began pulling plastic cards out of his wallet, blue and red and white cards, video membership cards and student cards and library cards, and shuffling through them as if he were about to find another insurance card. 'I know we're covered. Stop looking at me like that,' he nearly shouted at my mother, who did not stop looking at him.

'Oh, God,' she said in a tired voice. 'You're actually going to do this to us.'

'I don't see your names here,' the nurse said.

'Names,' my father said. 'Where don't you see our names?'

Nurse Douglas picked up the phone while he continued to study the computer screen in front of him. 'One moment,' he said. Behind him was a large black-and-white wall clock with a red second hand slowly ticking away. 'The computer is not always right,' Nurse Douglas said. It is not always right, I thought, and I tried to believe it was wrong now. But a voice in the telephone soon confirmed the opposite.

'I'm sure I paid,' my father said.

'Of course you did,' my mother said in a tone so cruel that I felt compelled to let go of her hand.

'Okay,' my father said to Nurse Douglas, 'if we have to, we can get on a payment plan. I'll pay some now and some later.' He counted through the cash in his wallet – a lot of ones and some fives. 'I can write a check.'

'One minute, please,' the nurse said. He left through a door behind his desk and did not return for a period of minutes, during which my father drummed his fingers on the desk.

'We're going to work this out,' he said, looking at my mother and me. 'This is not going to be a problem for us.'

When the nurse returned, he stood behind his desk. 'I'm sorry. I'm afraid we're overbooked tonight and won't have room for you.'

'You're joking,' my father said.

'You'll have to go to General. We've already called them. They're expecting you.'

'Look at him,' my father said, standing up now and pointing at me. He was a full head shorter than Nurse

Douglas and noticeably smaller. 'He's in pain and you're asking us to drive across town!'

'We can't treat him here. We're full.'

'Horseshit,' my father said. 'No one's here.' He pointed behind him at the waiting room. I noticed again that my father was wearing his flannel pajama top, that his Levis were old and worn, that he was no match in any way for Nurse Douglas. 'My son is in excruciating pain and your clinic is going to treat him.'

'I'm not. I'm not in that much pain,' I said. In fact, it hurt to say even those words. As I slowly stood up from my chair, I felt the muscles in my right side clench. But I wanted my father to lower his voice. I knew that the people in the waiting room were witnessing our humiliation, and I wanted to hurry out of that place.

'Mr. Parker,' Nurse Douglas said in a calm voice, 'we have called General. They know you're on your way. They're expecting you.'

My mother gestured to me then, and we headed back to the waiting room. 'Where are you going, Mary?' my father asked.

'To General,' she said.

'You stay right here,' he said. But we kept moving. 'Jesus,' he said. In the waiting room, the few families and elderly couples pretended not to notice my father, who was yelling at the nurse again. 'I've heard about this happening,' he was saying. 'On the news, on TV, in the papers. But I can't believe you're doing this to us.'

Jenny had stretched out over two seats and was

sleeping. 'What's wrong?' she asked when my mother woke her.

'Put your coat on. We're leaving.'

'Where's Dad?' she asked. 'What happened?'

'Shush,' my mother said.

Outside we waited for him in the car. It was completely dark now. The lighted windows of The Richmond Clinics were dim and blurred in the heavy snowfall. Sheets of white covered the parking lot and streets. 'We're going to somehow have to drive in this,' my mother said. We knew that we might have to wait a while since in situations of personal injustice my father did not relent easily. He would argue with that large, bearded nurse until he had exhausted himself and his sense of moral outrage and injury. We'd all seen him do it before over less: parking tickets, a drink on a restaurant bill that he'd insisted he'd never ordered. Once, for a period of weeks in Boise, he'd stopped at the telephone company after picking Jenny and me up from school to argue with them about having disconnected our phone. We always stayed in the car and had no idea what he could have been saying to them since our case had been very simple; we hadn't paid the phone bill in months. My father was unemployed then, and we simply couldn't afford to pay it. Still, he would fight. He did not have our sense of shame, and I knew even as I sat in pain in the cold car that I would have to be patient.

'Do you want me to go scream him out of there?' my mother asked. 'I will.'

'No,' I said. 'I'm okay.' I knew she didn't want to go back in there any more than I did.

'You're not okay,' she said. She looked at her watch. 'Your father is no good. No damn good.'

'Please don't say that,' I said, trying not to listen to her, trying to concentrate instead on the pain that was rising and falling inside me like a current now.

'Is your sister asleep?' she asked.

'I think so,' I said.

'When we're done taking care of you tonight, I'm leaving him.' She corrected herself. 'We're leaving him. Jenny, you, and me.'

She had said this before and not yet done it. But every time she said it, I believed that she would do it. And I believed her now. 'No,' I said.

'Yes,' she said. 'We're going to finally do what we should have done a long time ago. No more dragging our feet.'

'You can't do that,' I said, because I didn't know what else to say.

'I'm not the one who can't pay for your arm,' she said. 'I'm not the one who let our insurance lapse. I'm not the one who moved us out to this God-crazy city where the Mormons beat up my kids.' She was yelling, and Jenny moved a little and said a few indistinct words in her sleep, soft, dreamy, childlike utterances that made my mother's anger seem cruel and terribly adult. 'What did she say?' my mother asked, worried that Jenny might have been awake and listening. As the younger sibling – skinny and girlish – Jenny was treated like a kid; my mother and I had an unspoken agreement that she should be protected, that she should know none of my mother's worries. But she had heard nothing. She was curled up on her side of the backseat, breathing rhythmically, steadily, still fast asleep.

'She said that she doesn't want you to leave.'

My mother actually smiled. 'Stop that,' she said. 'I don't want to smile. Don't make me smile.' She tried to recover her sense of rage. 'We're leaving him. We're finally going to leave him.'

'My arm is killing me,' I said. 'Would you please go in there and get him.' But when we looked out the window, he was already there – marching across the parking lot.

'Here comes our hero,' my mother said. Snow fell into the car when he sat down and a cold wind blew in on us.

'We're going to General,' he said, the fight and anger still in his voice. He turned around and looked at me. 'Tomorrow I'm going to get us an attorney and I'm going to sue Nurse Douglas and The Richmond Clinics.' He looked out the windshield at the large battery of buildings, the hundreds of windows filled with distant light and glowing in the dark. 'I'm going to sue them. Big time,' he said.

My mother took out a cigarette and lit it. 'Steven and I have talked it over,' she said. 'We're leaving you. Me and the kids.'

'I see,' he said, not seeming very surprised.

'Tonight,' she said.

'Steven?' my father said without turning around to look at me.

'What?'

'Are you going to leave me tonight?'

I didn't say anything for a while. 'I don't know.'

'What?' he said.

'No. I'm not going to leave you.'

'And you, Jenny? Are you going to leave me?'

'She's asleep,' I said.

'Jenny,' he said. She moved a little.

'Leave her alone,' I said.

My father turned around in his seat and looked at me with what I thought was rage. For the first time I can remember, I expected him to hit me in the face, though he had never done so before. But then I saw in the gray shadows of the car that it was not rage he felt; it was confusion and maybe shame. 'Please don't talk to me like that, son,' he said. He turned back around. 'Okay,' he said in a calm voice, 'if you're going to leave me, where do you plan to go?'

'A friend's house,' my mother said.

'A friend's house,' my father repeated. 'You don't have any friends in Salt Lake.'

'Sure I do,' she said. We all knew that she didn't. We'd been there for only two months, and my parents were as friendless as Jenny and me. 'Or a motel. We'll go to a motel.'

'How are you planning to pay for a motel?'

'Somehow,' my mother said, though it was obvious that she had already lost her case. It was obvious that we had all lost that day. I had been unable to fight off a fat Mormon boy. My father had been powerless against Nurse Douglas and The Richmond Clinics. And my mother could not choose to leave my father. We were the kind of people who lost. Every day we lost, and I was exhausted by losing and hated it.

'Please,' I said not very loudly in the dark backseat of the car. 'My goddamn arm is killing me. Please take me to the hospital now.'

Salt Lake General was on the other side of town and would not be easy to reach in the blizzard. My father bent over the wheel and drove slowly, concentrating on the snow-covered road in front of him. We had an old Buick, which my father had bought from an elderly lady in Boise. A classic cream puff. But it had rear-wheel drive; and despite the sand bags my father had put in the trunk, it was fishtailing and sliding. We seemed to be the only car out in that weather. I held my arm and looked down cross streets for signs of anyone else. But I saw only the snow-covered shapes of parked automobiles. The glow from streetlamps passed in and out of the car so that I could see Jenny curled up beside me and sleeping. Dots of reflected light, filtered through the snow, fell over her. The pain had become familiar to me by then – a constant buzz that, now and then, when I breathed in too deeply, became suddenly piercing. 'God,' I moaned once when my father hit a bump.

Jenny woke, sat up, and looked around her. 'Can we talk about our house again?'

'Not now,' my father said.

'I'm scared,' she said.

'There's no reason to be scared,' he said. 'No reason in the world. Lie down and go back to sleep, kiddo.' She did just that, curling into a tight ball and nudging her head into my leg and in seconds falling into a deep, steady sleep while I stayed awake with my pain and looked out the windows at the storm, afraid and knowing beyond a doubt that there was every reason in the world to be afraid. Once we were swept as if by a strong wind off the road, straddled the curb, and knocked over a short row of garbage cans before we were just as suddenly flung back onto the road. My mother screamed and held on to my father. 'It's all right,' he said. 'Nothing happened.' And he kept on driving as if in fact nothing had. My mother demanded that we get on the interstate, which she thought would be plowed. But after we had spun our wheels all the way up the on-ramp, we pulled onto a wide, laneless ribbon of snow as far as we could see. 'Jesus,' my father said. 'Where are the fucking plows?' For the first time that night, I heard fear in his voice, fear and disbelief. All the same, he kept on driving, if still more slowly now, and I tried to think of the house up the hill that wasn't ours, the bathroom across from my room, the long, hushed hallways, the indoor pool. But I couldn't hold on to that picture, I couldn't see a damn thing, and my mother had begun to panic. 'We've got to stop,' she said.

'Stop where?' my father asked.

'We've got to get off this road and call the hospital and tell them to come get Steven.'

'Nobody's going to come get him,' my father said. He must have realized how much his statement had scared me since he now addressed me in the rearview mirror. 'How you holding up?'

'Shitty,' I said. 'I'm shitty.'

'Things will turn out just fine,' he said. 'We're almost there.'

I knew then that the pain I suffered through was pain he had inflicted on me, and I hated him for it. 'Why didn't you pay? Why didn't you pay the insurance?'

When he didn't respond, my mother said, 'Would you please give your son an explanation.'

It seemed like a very long time before he finally said, 'I'm sorry,' in a tone so full of misery and self-pity that I could no longer punish him.

Jenny sat up and said in a voice muted by whatever she had just been dreaming, 'Why don't we believe in God?'

'Shush,' my mother said. 'We're almost there. Go back to sleep now.' And Jenny, with her remarkable ability to obey, once again lay down and slept.

When we finally got to General, the parking lot was full and my father drove up to the emergency room entrance where, before he let us out, he turned around and looked at me. 'When this is all done,' he said, 'we're going to teach you how to fight. We'll get you lessons or training – whatever it takes. Next time this happens, you're going to pull that kid's arm out of joint.'

I was surprised at the anger in his voice, and for some reason I felt that I should say something. 'Okay,' I said.

He took a large breath. 'But right now we're going to have to change our plan. We're going to have to calm down and do what's best for ourselves. You with me?'

'Yes,' I said, though I didn't really understand him.

'Good. So who did this to you? What's his name?'

'No one,' I said. 'I already told you, it was an accident. I was playing football.'

'I thought you said you were with me, Steven. Besides, we all know you don't play football.'

'Yes, I do.'

'Steven,' my father said.

'I know who did it.' Jenny sat up in her seat.

'No, you don't,' I said. I was pretty sure that she didn't. Jenny and I knew no one.

'I do! I do!' she said, as if she had a great deal to prove to all of us. 'His name is Danny Olsen. He has one younger brother and three older sisters and lives up the hill from us on Honeycomb Drive.'

'That's not him,' I said, though from the tone of her voice, I could tell she had told the truth. 'How do you know that?'

'I just do,' she said, smiling.

'What are you going to do?' I asked my father. 'You can't call his house. You can't.'

My father had turned back around in his seat, and my mother got out and opened the door for me. 'Let's go,

Steven,' she said. I wanted to refuse to leave the car and fight my father and his plan. But as soon as my mother reached out to me and said, 'Let's get you taken care of, kiddo,' I knew I'd do anything to stop the pain.

The emergency room at General was crowded and loud. The white linoleum floor was streaked with muddy, latticed shoe prints, and little yellow triangles placed at intervals said CAUTION WET FLOORS! Patients and their families sat in simple plastic chairs, the chrome legs of which screeched against the linoleum. Magazines lay on the floor, their pages torn where people had stepped on them. 'I liked the other hospital better,' Jenny said. 'Why didn't we stay there?' My mother sent Jenny to find a place for us to sit in the crowded reception area while we waited in a line with other injured people, at the head of which a policeman stood. Voices spoke to each other in the walkie-talkie on his belt.

My mother put her hand on my good shoulder. 'We're almost there,' she said.

I felt another hand – icy cold – on my neck and looked up at my father. 'We're going to teach you how to fight. I promise. You won't have to go through this again.'

'I fought,' I said. 'I tried.'

'Sure you did,' he said. 'You're going to have to tell the truth now, Steven. You understand?' He was no longer angry. He was intense, directed, and anxious, as if he himself were about to enter the ring and fight.

'I'll try,' I said.

'Good boy.'

When we reached the head of the line, my father told the nurse that he wanted to speak to the police. 'My son has been assaulted,' he said. Almost immediately, a policeman came. The tag on his chest pocket read FRANKS, and he was a large, blond man with a beard who, I realized, closely resembled Nurse Douglas. 'I want to press charges against the kid who did this to my son.'

'We'll have to ask your son some questions,' Franks said.

'Whatever it takes to get a little justice done,' my father said. I could tell that Franks did not like my father, did not care for his sense of entitlement, his loud demand for justice.

Franks looked at me. 'He seems a little tired. Maybe we should wait until they've treated him. Maybe we should give him a little time.'

'I think we're ready to do this now,' my father said.

I don't remember the questions that Officer Franks asked me, though I could tell by the way my father stood – his arms crossed, his face calm, unmoved, determined – that my answers pleased him, that he believed his plan was working. As I talked, I looked at Franks's belt, the heavy black gun in its holster, the black club dangling down the length of his thigh. I heard my mother talking to someone. 'Could we get something for the pain? He's in terrible pain.' After the questioning was done, a nurse offered me two bright pink capsules. 'These should help,' she said. 'They might make you float a little.' I was standing on a scale in a back room. The brightness of the light hurt my eyes. The nurse gave me a little Dixie cup of water with the pills. 'He's number fifteen on the list,' she said to my mother.

Out in the lobby I began to feel weightless and good, and leaned up against the side of the Coca-Cola machine next to me – glowing red and humming from within – and fell asleep. When I woke, Jenny was talking to an Asian girl who was holding a washcloth to her hand. Her mother held a baby, lost in a bundle of pink and white blankets, and yelled in a language I didn't understand at her little boy, who was kicking an aluminum can across the muddy floor. 'Say the word *Coca-Cola* in Vietnamese,' Jenny was saying to the injured girl.

'I don't know it in Vietnamese,' the girl said.

'They're number seventeen,' Jenny said to me. 'We're two numbers before them.' I was groggy from those pills and wasn't sure what my sister meant. 'Say "Coke is it!" in your language,' Jenny politely demanded. The girl said something then, though the only word I understood was *Coke*. The woman with the baby leaned over and shouted something to her daughter in Vietnamese that made the girl turn away from us and read a book she'd had in her lap.

Jenny looked over at me. 'I'm bored,' she said. Next to Jenny, my mother had fallen asleep in her chair. I had no idea where my father could be. 'This is taking forever.' I looked down at my arm, studying the odd way my palm and elbow pointed away from my body. 'Does it really,

really hurt?' Jenny asked.

'It's not so bad with these pills,' I said. I was able to sit up straighter, and my breathing was easier, though any sudden movement sent a stab of pain along my right side. 'How did you know his name?' I asked. 'How did you know he's Danny Olsen?'

'From last year's yearbook,' she said. 'I memorized some names in it.'

'Why?' I asked.

'Just because,' she said. 'I know every kid in last year's tenth grade. One hundred and twenty-three kids.'

'You don't know them,' I said.

'I know their names,' she said.

'Those kids are going to hate us now, you know. They're always going to hate us.'

'Maybe not.' She looked over at my mother and said, 'She's going to leave, isn't she?'

'What?' I said. 'Who's going to leave?'

'I'm not stupid. I heard you two talking in the car. I always hear that stuff.'

'You're not supposed to know that,' I said.

'Is she going to leave?' Jenny asked, this time in her little-girl voice, the one she used when she wanted something or when she was frightened. 'Do you think she would do that?'

'Shush. She'll hear us.'

'No, she won't,' Jenny said. 'She's sleeping.'

I looked over at my mother, who was leaning her head against the wall behind her. Her eyes moved beneath her closed lids, and her mouth was cocked open in a way that made her seem vulnerable and very distant, and it made me feel that I should look away from her, which I did. 'I don't know,' I said. 'I don't know what she's going to do.'

'Yes, you do,' Jenny said.

She was scared now, honestly scared, and just wanted me to say something that would make her feel safe. 'No,' I said, 'I don't think she will. She always says she's going to, but she never does.' That's not what I felt. But it's what I knew I had to say, even if I was in no mood to pretend, even if I was tired of being alone with what I thought I knew.

'Good,' Jenny said. She looked away from me and began paging through another magazine, reading about what women do to make themselves pretty and attractive to men. She sighed. 'I'm bored. Bored, bored, bored.' I was glad that, for now, she was done feeling scared, and I could barely keep my eyes open. 'Sleepy boy,' she said, smiling at me and touching my hair.

'Could you get my glasses out of my pocket for me?' I asked. I had just noticed that everything in the distance – the walls, the people, the reception desk – was blurry, that I had to squint to see things. Jenny handed my glasses to me, and I put them on only to find that the left lens had broken so that I saw the walls, chairs, magazines, and muddy floors of that room very clearly broken into two pieces. 'Jesus,' I whispered, because I'd wanted to feel that I had at least saved one small thing from that stupid day.

'Go to sleep now,' Jenny said. And I closed my eyes on the broken picture in front of me and slept.

When I woke again, my entire right side was on fire. 'We're up,' my mother said. 'It's our turn.'

'The pills stopped working,' I said.

'Okay,' she said. 'He says the pills stopped working.' She was talking to the attendant. Jenny was walking behind me. Behind her, my father stood at the Coke machine talking to a man in a suit and tie.

'Is Dad coming with us?' I asked.

'I'll be there in a minute, Steven,' he said. 'One minute.'

The attendant left us in a little room, where I sat up on a sort of bed and looked at a chart of human anatomy on the wall, dozens of multicolored organs stuck to a man's skeletal frame. The sight of it made me think about how disgusting and unimaginably complicated people are inside. 'Stop playing with that,' my mother snapped at Jenny, who was fiddling with something on her side of the room. My mother was looking at her watch when a young woman came in followed by a short, muscular man who pushed a metal cart. 'I'm Dr. Gardener,' the woman said, already looking at my shoulder. 'This is Martin. He's going to help us put your arm back into joint.' She was short and had a wide nose and small, pointy breasts inside her white lab coat. I wanted her to be more attractive. She cut my T-shirt off with large scissors that felt icy against my skin. 'You're spasming,' the doctor said. 'That's normal. What would you say, Martin?' Dr. Gardener asked.

'That's a dislocation, all right,' Martin said. I looked down at it and saw the muscle quivering beneath the tight skin. Martin smiled at me. 'It won't be as bad as you think. Best thing about it is it's quick. As fast as you can snap your fingers.' He snapped his fingers. I looked back down at my shoulder and noticed the unnatural round bone poking up beside my clavicle. 'That's a doozy. You get ten points for that,' he said, trying to be funny. 'You might have some tissue damage, too.'

Martin left the room to fetch an IV drip that, as Dr. Gardener explained to me, was going to make me drowsy. 'We wouldn't want you to be wide awake for this,' she said.

But when Martin returned, he didn't have an IV. The IV would have to come from another hospital across town. We could wait, but there was no telling how long it would take, given the weather. 'I'm sorry to say,' Martin said.

'I want to go to sleep,' I said.

'I think you're going to be better off getting this over with, Steven,' Dr. Gardener said. She was removing the plastic guard from the needle of a large syringe. 'This will relax those muscles and make this a little more comfortable for you,' she said.

'I'm not going to look,' I heard my sister say.

'Where's my father?' I asked.

'I'll go get him,' my mother said, starting for the door.

'No,' I said. 'Don't leave.'

'You might feel a small prick.' When Dr. Gardener thrust the needle into my shoulder and began counting slowly to ten, I looked away and saw Jenny staring at the thing that was happening to me. She was biting her thumb.

'Stop looking at me,' I said.

'Hold tight,' Dr. Gardener said. She had finished with the needle and was now placing my good arm around her neck and embracing me, holding me so close that I smelled the warm, salty stink of her skin. My right arm had gone almost completely numb. 'I'm not going to tell you that this won't be a little uncomfortable, but it will only last a moment or two. That's a promise.'

'I wish I could sleep,' I said. I closed my eyes, but I couldn't keep them closed. I wanted to see what they were doing to me.

'This will help us get some leverage,' Martin said. He began wrapping a white sheet around my arm. 'This will only take a second.' He was still adjusting the sheet, tightening it like a sort of sock around my arm.

'I'm not ready,' I said.

'Think good thoughts,' Martin said. 'Think of something you like. Concentrate real hard on it. All right?'

'Please wait,' I said because nothing good had occurred to me, because I needed more time to think of something. But Martin had already stepped back; a moment later, I knew only that Dr. Gardener was still holding me and that I was screaming at the top of my lungs.

★

I didn't want the wheelchair, but the doctor insisted that I sit in it at least for the initial trip down the hall. There were other patients in wheelchairs – an old lady in a pink robe, a little kid in striped pajamas who sucked on his fingers and looked scared. Jenny pushed me through this strange traffic of sick people while my mother walked behind us and quietly talked with the doctor.

'Do you know where we're going next?' Jenny asked.

'I don't really care,' I said.

'Danny Olsen and his father are here,' she said. 'I saw them. Danny Olsen's been crying. You can tell. We're going to meet them in the cafeteria now. He's supposed to apologize to you.' After they had put my arm back into joint, Jenny must have slipped out of the room and done some snooping around. 'Dad's threatening to sue them or something. I heard him talking on the phone before.'

'What?' I said.

'He was asking for money to pay for the hospital bills . . . to pay for your suffering and inconvenience.'

'You shouldn't know that,' I said. I was really seeing that night how much my little sister knew and tried to know, how much she made it her business to know. 'You shouldn't know any of that.' I couldn't help feeling that I shouldn't, either, that neither of us should.

My father walked up behind us. 'Let me take him for a minute, Jen-Jen,' he said. I could tell he was in a good mood. His voice sounded upbeat, happy, large. Jenny let go of my chair and ran down the hallway.

'Don't run!' my father shouted after her, but she kept on running. 'How's your arm, Steven?'

'I know what you're doing,' I said. 'I know you're trying to get money from them.'

My father slowed his pace. 'Yes, I am,' he said. 'Is that such a bad thing?'

'Yes,' I said. 'It's a bad thing.'

'I thought you would be happy. That kid hurt you. We're getting him back. We're going to win this thing.'

'We're not winning,' I said.

'Yes, we are. They hurt us, and we're hurting them back.'

'They hurt *me*. I don't want to hurt anybody back.'

'You don't?' my father asked. 'You really don't?' I didn't say anything. 'I need to ask you something, Steven.'

'What?'

'We're meeting this boy and his father now. They've agreed to give us what we're asking. Things might have been a whole lot more difficult for us. But Mr. Olsen is ashamed of what happened, and he wants his son to see the pain and the suffering he's caused us. He wants his son to learn from this. And I want them to see that we're going to be gracious, that we're going to be good sports. I'd like you to give me your word that you'll be gracious.'

'No,' I said. 'Hell, no.'

My father stopped, locked the wheels of the chair, and kneeled down in front of me. 'How much do you think that's going to cost?' He gestured at my arm. 'You'll need to see a physical therapist for a month or two. You realize that something like that is outrageously expensive. How much do you think?'

I didn't want to look at him, but his face was too close to mine to avoid. 'A lot, I guess.'

'A whole lot,' he said.

'Times are good, aren't they? Soon we won't need to worry about money. That's what you always say.'

'I'm talking about now, Steven.'

'It's my stupid arm. Mine.'

'Of course it is,' he said, laughing a little. 'But someone has to pay for it.' We both looked down at my arm. It was in a sling and my fingers were swollen and red. It was numb and tingling and felt far away. 'That's why we're going after these people. All I need from you right now is a little good behavior. Can you give me that?'

I looked up at him, his eyes bloodshot but alert, awake. I felt sick to my stomach then, though not because of what my father was doing. I felt sick because I wanted to know something and had to ask him about it. 'How much are they going to give us? How much money?'

'Enough,' he said. 'More than enough.'

'Okay,' I said. 'I'll be a good sport.'

Jenny was sprinting down the hallway toward us, stupid and happy and flailing her arms. 'I get him back now!' she shouted. 'I get to push him again.'

The cafeteria was large and mostly empty and uncomfortably quiet. The warm, suffocating smell of mashed potatoes seemed to be everywhere, even though no one stood in the food line. Danny Olsen and his father sat at a large round table in the middle of the room. I couldn't see them too well because I wasn't wearing my broken glasses. (I didn't want that kid to know he had defeated me in this small way, too.) As we drew nearer, I saw that the father and son seemed to be looking at some difficult, invisible object at the center of the table. We came to a stop, they stood up, and I could see that Danny Olsen was frightened of the cripple in front of him, frightened of what he had done to me. His hair was still wet from a shower or bath he had recently taken, and his chubby face seemed too white and harshly scrubbed; and even though he was sort of fat, he looked small and shaken. Jenny locked the wheels of my chair in place and Mr. Olsen nodded at me. He wore a suit and his hair was nicely combed, and in his middle-aged, chubby face I easily saw the resemblance between father and son. 'Go ahead, Daniel,' he urged. My father stood off to the side of me, his arms folded. He wore a pleasant and somehow serious smile on his face. Despite his silly flannel pajama top, he was a capable-looking man with deep-set eyes and a nose that had been handsomely broken, set off slightly to one side. He looked strong and good-natured and, to use his word, gracious, more gracious than I knew him to be. I tried to stand up from my chair, but having only one good arm, slipped. When I tried again, I felt the surprising strength of Jenny's hand holding me down. 'Don't,' she said. 'You're not ready to stand yet.'

Danny Olsen looked at me. 'I'm sorry,' he said in a small voice.

'I want to hear it,' Mr. Olsen said.

'I'm sorry,' he said in a louder voice.

'And,' his father prompted.

Danny Olsen bit into his lower lip, looked down at the floor and then up at me again. 'I was in the wrong. I apologize for what I did to you. I apologize for what I said to you.'

'Go ahead, Daniel,' Mr. Olsen said. Danny Olsen put his trembling right hand out, which was confusing because I could only offer him my uninjured left. We grasped awkwardly at the other's mismatched hand and then quickly let go.

'We're not Catholic or anything,' I said.

My father cleared his voice behind me. 'Steven,' he said.

'Okay,' I said to Danny. 'Thanks for the apology.' Danny Olsen moved his arms from his pockets, crossed them, let one dangle. He felt awkward and ashamed, looking down at me in my wheelchair, and I knew that we had won, that that moment was my family's moment of victory, and I tried to feel whatever emotions – elation, superiority, graciousness – winners are supposed to feel. But I didn't feel those things. Instead, I felt satisfied to see that the kid who had hurt me was scared. I felt safe knowing that they were not only going to give us the money we needed, but also more than we needed, more than enough. I was pretty sure that this was not the feeling of winners. I was pretty sure that this was not 'graciousness'. It was too greedy and mean for that.

Jenny stepped in front of my chair and put out her hand just as Danny Olsen had been about to turn around. 'I'm Steven's sister, Jenny,' she said. 'It's nice to meet you.'

He didn't turn to meet her at first, and I thought about how this was her chance to speak with one of the hundreds of names she had memorized from the yearbook. I hoped that he would be kind to her. 'Daniel,' his father said sternly, after which he relented and, without looking her in the eye, briefly touched my sister's hand.

Later that night, after Mr. Olsen and his son had left and after my father had written a check to the hospital for the amount in full, a check he knew would not bounce, winning began to feel like something real and substantial, something that stayed with you and changed you and your life for good. It was past one in the morning when we finally drove away from the hospital. The snow had eased off by then, the roads had been plowed, and driving was easier. Jenny, who had always had a funny and demanding appetite, announced from the backseat that she was hungry. 'I want an ice cream,' she said.

'I don't see why we shouldn't celebrate,' my father said. Perhaps had I not been on muscle relaxants, had it not been early in the morning, my father's use of the word *celebrate* on that occasion might have seemed odd to me. But at that moment, it seemed right, and we stopped and were soon all feasting on ice-cream bars in the parking lot of a Gas-N-Go. None of us laughed at or even noticed our odd choice of frozen desserts in the middle of winter and in the aftermath of a blizzard. We simply ate as the car heater blasted warm air and the windows around us fogged up.

For the rest of the drive home, my mother leaned into my father and whispered to him. I could not hear her, but I knew by the way he kissed her on the cheek and she returned his kiss that they were both happy. I think that she must have believed in him that night. I know I did. I know also that she must have seen, as I saw, that my father, for all his rage and past failures, could be a strong man, a man who knew, one way or another, how to get what he wanted. In fact, as we all saw a week later, when new furniture arrived, when the pissy-smelling La-Z-Boy disappeared from our rented duplex, when we were able to replace my eyeglasses with a new pair – new frames and new lenses – he had gotten more than enough, and at, or so I believed that night, a pretty good price – the price of a little pain, an injury, some tears and aggravation, a quarrel among kids. And as we drove across the city and my mother fell asleep and Jenny curled up on her side of the seat and dozed, I hardly remembered the pain. It had been masked and smothered beneath the medicine and the victory. For once, I believed that the future would be better and larger than I had ever before let myself imagine it could be. I knew how it felt to win. I knew that believing – and not just pretending – that the next day would be better than the present one was the conviction of winners. It was a boom time, and soon we'd be in the middle of it. I had not felt this way much before; it was a feeling that made that night remarkable with possibility, a night on which I had begun to see a future that held the promise of something as miraculous and unbelievable as an indoor pool, a warm swim in the middle of winter, in a blizzard on a night like that night. I could see that pool then, imagine myself walking from the dry carpet of the living room into the strange, damp enclosure where aquatic shadows flitted over the walls and where I stood and heard the wet suck of filters as I looked through the glassy slab of water and made out in the deep end the little silver coin of the drain at the bottom. A real pool.

'Steven,' my father whispered. 'You awake?'

'Yes,' I said.

'You did well tonight. You hung in there.'

'Thanks,' I said.

'You know how to throw a left hook?' he asked. Before I could answer, he began to tell me. 'Don't telegraph it. You don't want the other guy to know what's coming. You want to step into it. You've got to be fast.' He threw a couple punches just short of the wind-shield, and with my good arm I threw two or three, despite the fact that it hurt a little. 'Good,' he said, though he couldn't have been watching me closely. 'That's the idea. We're going to teach you how to fight,' he said, still boxing. 'We're going to make a fighter out of you.'

'Great,' I said, believing him, absolutely believing him, as I threw another two punches into the dark air in front of me.

2

I had never seen my family spend more money than in the month after my accident. It was February and what the Channel 2 weatherman called an inversion – a soupy, dirty smog – had settled over the Salt Lake Valley and would probably stay for weeks. The sky and the ring of white mountains around the city disappeared in the murky brown air. Mornings at the bus stop were strange and a little spooky as the headlights of invisible cars pushed through the thick air and drove past us. My arm was still in a sling, and when Jenny and I walked to the back of the bus and past the boys who'd hurt me – Danny Olsen among them – they became quiet and looked away. We had gone from being outcasts to being unseen. My arm would not heal quickly, the doctors had told me; along with the dislocation, my muscle and some ligaments had been torn and damaged. I struggled to do schoolwork with my left hand, took vitamin supplements, and went weekly to The Richmond Clinics – where I was treated now that Mr. Olsen was paying the bill – for physical therapy.

Despite my arm and the bleak season, those few weeks of sudden riches were reminiscent of better times for our family. Our best time was the first year in Boise when my father had been the manager of a windshield replacement business, had liked his job and the people he worked with. My mother had found a nice house for us to rent. It was small, but it had new wood floors and the fuses wouldn't short when you toasted bread and brewed coffee at the same time. The owners, an old couple called the Brownings – related, my father claimed, to the family who sold the guns of that name – even talked about selling that house to us. My father and mother made friends, Mr. and Mrs. Kirkeby from across the street and Joel and his live-in girlfriend, Christina, who lived a couple streets down from us. My mother thought of returning to nursing school and taking a part-time job until she finished her degree. Both Jenny and I liked our school and had the sense that for once we would stay in a place for more than two years, maybe stay there for good. It was a nice thing to believe after having changed schools several times, moving from California to Arizona, then back to California, from where we moved once more to Washington State, and finally to Boise. We'd had good times in those places, too, though they hadn't lasted long. My father had had repeated bad luck and always knew an old friend in another state who had a job for him. When that golden year in Boise came to an end, we stayed another year before we moved on to Salt Lake, where, even if we didn't have friends, we could start again. I think we all hoped our unusual beginning in Salt Lake would put us on that same good track and keep us there. We had money, at least, and wouldn't have to worry for a change about how to pay the bills that winter and, I hoped, for many winters to come.

The things our new money bought made my family giddy for a while – the matching couch and La-Z-Boy, the new TV with stereo sound, black and sleek, so shiny it glinted with the flash of your reflection whenever you walked by, the new Danish blue dishes for my mother, some pots and pans, a set of kitchen knives in a knife block, a new pair of eyeglasses with silver frames for me. The chair and couch were red and had been carried in by two men from a place called Instant Furniture, which was printed on their white monkey suits and in giant letters on the side of their truck. It was instant, too, miraculously there, in the middle of our small home, packed in thick plastic that Jenny and I tore off until we got to the fabric that smelled new – of detergent and untouched cloth and of fresh-cut wood beneath the thick stuffing. We subscribed to more than sixty cable channels, including the ones you paid extra for – MTV, HBO, The Romance Station, and even a channel called Play It Again that featured reruns of *Gilligan's Island, Bewitched*, and *I Dream of Jeannie*. Jenny and I lay on the couch and surfed the channels for hours, fighting over the remote control, over which program to watch, until our eyes felt sore and our mother said no more TV and sent us to our rooms, exhausted and lethargic from doing what she called too much of nothing.

After a while, my father began to bring home stuff nobody wanted or needed. He bought a new basketball for me, even though I had an old one that I never used. 'Smell that leather,' he said. I did smell it, though I couldn't hide my lack of excitement. (I had never been particularly good at hiding anything.) 'You don't like it,' he said.

'Sure I do.'

'I'd appreciate some gratitude. A thank-you, at least.'

'Thank you,' I said.

'You're welcome,' he said in a tone that let me know I had disappointed him.

My sister and mother were even less receptive to his misfired attempts to please. When he gave Jenny a stack of CDs by Billy Joel, she said, 'That's what I liked last year. I don't listen to him anymore. Why don't you ask me what I want?'

'You're very welcome,' he said.

To the candles and perfumes, soaps and cosmetics he gave my mother, she smiled. 'Thank you, Billy,' she said. 'But we don't need these things.' More than once, my mother and Jenny and I drove from store to store – sometimes as many as six – returning expensive bubble baths, incense sticks, a lava lamp, sea sponges, costume jewelry, chocolates, and sweets. When the sales people sometimes refused to accept the returns, my mother argued vehemently until they relented. 'My husband bought these things,' she'd say, becoming fiercely honest. 'But we can't pay for them. We are not the kind of family who can afford fifteen-dollar bubble bath.'

The salesperson would then eye Jenny and me, seeming to confirm what kind of family we were, before finally saying, 'All right, then. Just this once.'

My father had never cared for shopping, especially grocery shopping. But for the four short weeks of that February during which the Salt Lake Valley was covered in the dirty muck of inversion and the nights were black and starless and the lights of the city, even when you looked from the top of the Downs, became distant, blurry, and disconnected dots lost in the swampy air, my father was determined to make a sort of party out of our weekly trips to the Albertson's Super Store. 'I'm going to let the kids loose on the cookie aisle. You've got ten seconds to grab whatever you want.' It was for events like these that he had persuaded Jenny and me, who'd rarely accompanied my mother on shopping trips before, to climb into the Buick and drive through the black smog – the air made two smoky cones in our headlights – for an evening of family food shopping. My father didn't seem to understand that I was too old to freak out with happiness – which he wanted to see us do – over a timed rush at the cookie, cold cereal, or candy aisle. But Jenny was still willing to act the part of a kid and go spastic, become giggly and greedy, as she filled her arms full of

Keebler Fudge Shoppe Fudge Sticks, Chips Ahoy!, and Chips Deluxe, Fudge Shoppe Deluxe Grahams, and Pecan shortbread Sandies, and whatever else she could grab and haul to our shopping cart before my father – attracting the attention of other shoppers and store employees – eyed his wristwatch and shouted, 'Time!' When my mother complained, when she called it wasteful, accused him of spoiling his daughter, when she said we couldn't afford to play with food, my father claimed it was just this once, though he'd do it again the following week.

I think she, as I did, half liked to see him make Jenny run wild, arms full of needless things my sister and I and maybe even my mother and father had never tasted. For my mother, shopping had always been a tedious process of price comparisons and coupon clippings, which she kept in an envelope taped to the refrigerator door. My father was quick and careless. He tossed cans and boxes, fresh pastas and sauces, cheeses, pâtés, and spreads we'd never tried – and later found stinky, uneatable, and threw away – into the cart without looking at prices. She'd never shopped that way. None of us had. As soon as my father convinced her that it was just this once – 'Let's treat ourselves, for God's sake!' – or that this, he promised, was the last time, no more after this, she calmed down, relaxed, even began to eye the shelves and claim a few items – a bottle of red wine vinegar, flavored olive oil, fresh strawberries – for herself.

The store was different for shoppers who could buy

what they wanted. My father hummed to the old music –
'Respect', 'Your Kiss Is on My List', 'Blue Skies' – that
played in the store, kicking a foot, moving his hips a little,
performing a small dance move. In the produce section,
hidden sprinklers sprayed silver mists of water over the
vegetables while a voice over the intercom – happy and
confirming – announced special sale items, which we no
longer had to consider buying. My sister tackled my
father, hanging off him and begging for something she'd
just seen. 'Can I? Can I? Please . . . please.'

'Why not?' he'd say.

I remember something odd about that particular
supermarket. A family of birds lived in there that winter,
quick little field sparrows. You'd see one shoot across the
fluorescent sky inside that store, and all you could do was
laugh. Another perched for an instant on the exit sign
above the sliding doors before bolting off again. Jenny
called them the Bird family, even though I told her birds
didn't have families, at least in the sense that she was
thinking when she called them Mr. and Mrs. Bird. They
lived well in that universe of shelved food. Once we saw
one flit over the cold cereal aisle, land where a box of
Cocoa Puffs had burst open over the floor, and rapidly
feed on the chocolate debris before an Albertson's em-
ployee rushed it with a net. It easily escaped, flew off,
landed again, pecked at the chocolate cereal, and then
again shot off before the empty net landed. We cham-
pioned the birds. 'You've got to survive somehow,' my
father said.

Once they did catch one. We didn't see it happen. We just saw a short man walking quickly through the produce section holding up a meshed canvas cage in which a sparrow fluttered. The man was bald and pale and wore a latex glove on the hand he held the cage with. Jenny and I followed him and tried to look in at the bird, which the man didn't particularly like. 'Excuse me,' he said. He was a small man, with a mustache the same shade of gray as the bird he had trapped. His eyes were pink and darted quickly at and then away from us, after which he seemed to look at us from the side of his face.

'How'd you catch it?' I asked.

'A trap,' he said.

'Is it a boy or a girl?' Jenny asked.

'Neither,' he said. 'It's a female. A hen.'

'It's Mrs. Bird,' Jenny said.

We followed him out to the parking lot where a light crystalline snow fell. It was freezing, and the cold seemed to drive the bird into a frenzied twirping. 'What's wrong with him?' Jenny asked.

'Not *he*,' he said. '*She*.' The man actually glanced at us then. 'I'd guess she wants to go back inside,' he said. 'There's more food in there, isn't there?'

Jenny actually answered him. 'Yes.'

'Why are you wearing that glove?' I asked him.

'Birds are extremely dirty.' He opened the flap in the canvas and the sparrow shot out into the dark and was gone. 'I've got to go back in there now and handle food, after all, don't I?'

Ten minutes later, Jenny and I saw him in the produce section arranging oranges in a pyramid, examining the bagged lettuce, eyeing the zucchinis, and Jenny said in her little girl's voice, 'Poor Mrs. Bird'. I also tried to feel bad for it, Mrs. Bird out in the cold dark winter with nowhere to go. But it was really just a hen, as the produce man had said, a dirty animal, and you couldn't think too much about a dirty bird when what you really wanted to do was reach into the large, round bins of candy advertising three items for $.89 – three Twix bars, three Snickers, three 3 Musketeers, three Chunky bars, three Kit Kats, three Reese's Peanut Butter Cups, three bags of Peanut M&M's – three of anything you wanted for less than a dollar. We'd never bought candy before that February, before what my family had come to call my accident. Candy, sweet cereals, Pop-Tarts, cookies, ice cream, and frozen desserts were new to Jenny and me. During those few weeks, these sweet, useless foods meant we had become rich. We could have as much as we wanted when we wanted it, though buying it was always better than eating it. At home, only minutes after unbagging the groceries, we broke open the Chips Deluxe, the Kit Kat bars, the Pecan shortbread Sandies, the chocolate-covered graham crackers, and ate until exhausted, until the chocolate tasted waxy and our mouths, full of shortbread, lined with flour and sugar, dried out, until we felt stuffed, if not quite sick, until the bored, draining sensation of satisfaction left us calm, let down, and looking for something else to think about and desire.

Those shopping trips stopped all at once at the end of February, not because my mother put a stop to them or even because we ran out of money, but simply because they were no longer enough, no longer interesting, no longer worth the trip to the store. They stopped because food was just food, and you could eat only so much of it before it got stale in your mouth, before you got sick of the taste of it and threw it away. They stopped in the middle of winter when it was cold and the nights were short and the gray inversion still clung to the valley and we wondered what could be next for us and hoped that it would be more than excessive food shopping, that it would be something that would change us, something that we not only wanted before we got it, but that we would keep on wanting afterwards, too, something that would make all the wanting and dreaming that had come before seem worth it, more than worth it, even.

3

The day in late February when I was supposed to have my sling removed began with a fight over my sister's hair. Jenny was used to getting what she wanted. Most recently, she had received the outfit that she was wearing that morning – the expensive purple Keds, a purple blouse and khaki pants from the Gap, and the translucent, purple, waterproof Swatch watch from a store in Crossroads Mall called In Excess, the sort of store our family could not afford. The watch had been at the bottom of a fish tank half-buried in little colored rocks as exotic fish swam above it. 'Can I, please?' she had begged my father. '*Please, please, please!*' He could not say no, even to an eighty-dollar plastic watch. And so she was given that, too. As far as I was concerned, my arm had bought her an entire far-too-pricey wardrobe – her green and yellow and pink polo shirts, her jeans and pants that had to be from the Gap. And that morning, she wanted our mother to do her hair, despite the fact that our mother was about to be late for her new job at Oak Groves Assisted Living, where she fed and bathed old people forty hours a week, and had already shouted down the hall that she could not, absolutely not, be late for work again if we wanted to have food on our table. She'd taken the job a month ago, right after my injury, so that our family could have full-coverage medical insurance. She was a nurse's aide, and did whatever duties the doctors and nurses weren't willing to do. It was the sort of job that was difficult to fill and that no one wanted, which was why the benefits were good and the pay wasn't bad. She'd probably gotten it because she'd finished a year of nursing school when she was nineteen or twenty and because nobody more qualified had applied for it. 'Please! Please!' Jenny shouted through the cracked bathroom door until my mother rushed out of her room with her nurse's white blouse half undone so that, eating my toast in the kitchen, I had to look away from the site of her bra, the textured lace of it, and had to put that image out of my mind.

'Will you please cooperate for once?' She shouted out the word *cooperate* in this long, desperate way.

Just as my mother turned around and headed back to her room, Jenny shoved her face out the bathroom door. 'What am I supposed to do with this? I can't go like this. Nobody even cares.' She let her hair drop. She shook it the way a wet dog does, water flying out into the air. She had tryouts for the Billmore drill team that afternoon and wanted to look her best.

'It's just your stupid hair,' I said.

'What can I do? I'll do something,' my father said because he hated it when Jenny threw a tantrum. Her moods really worked on him. They really upset him. He stood from the breakfast table with melted butter from his toast shining on his fingertips and walked over to the bathroom where Jenny slammed the door on him. 'I'll help, sweetie.'

'You can't help. Only Mom can help.'

'She says only you can help!' my father shouted down the hall to my mother.

'She's doing this on purpose,' I said.

When my mother didn't respond, Jenny said, 'Get her for me, please.' Her voice came through the door in a long, pink, soft hush that my mother had somehow heard down the hall.

'All right,' she said, bolting out of her room, her white blouse still half open so that once again I had to look away, though not before I saw the strained cords in her neck, the soft strokes of her clavicles, the lacy cups of her bra and the little white silk bow poised delicately above her sternum. Seeing that bothered me. I don't think I ever desired my mother in a way that I had to feel ashamed of. I understood that she was a woman as well as my mother. But I also knew that in other families mothers did not walk through the hallway in half-rages with their blouses open. I knew that in other families sons did not have to look away, did not have to erase the picture in their heads of the little white bow.

'I'm here,' she said to the closed bathroom door, and Jenny opened it and looked at her with vulnerable eyes that anticipated a harsh reaction and stopped it before it could happen. 'Just give me a comb and barrettes,' my mother said with a great deal of resignation, and for the next fifteen minutes my mother worked Jenny's hair into a subtle, tight crown of cuteness, combing, curling, blow-drying, tucking strands in, pinning and tying off two ribbons and clipping down a translucent purple barrette that matched her Swatch watch perfectly. 'There,' my mother said, though of course she would be late again that day and our insurance, our ability to pay bills, to put food on the table, to put gas in the car and clothes on our backs would once again be threatened.

'Thank you,' Jenny said.

'You're welcome,' my mother said, looking into the mirror at Jenny. From where I sat at the kitchen table, I could not see the mirror or Jenny, but I could see the concern on my mother's face. Then, for some reason, she bent down, kissed Jenny on the cheek, and said, 'You know that I love you, don't you?' It was a weird thing for her to say, not only because she said it – which she did often enough – but also because she should have been in a hurry and because she touched my sister's cheek and waited for Jenny to look at her and say yes, she knew. Of course she knew. 'Good,' my mother said. 'Because I do. More than you can know, I do.'

After school that day, I went to Jenny's tryout, which

she'd begged me to watch, and was shocked to see that Jenny really did have talent. In the last month, my sister had blossomed so fast that at times she no longer felt like my kid sister. I certainly couldn't have guessed when the physical part had happened to her, though somehow it had. She shot up at least an inch and got teacup breasts about the same time I began to notice the lattice of bra straps through her T-shirts and her Gap blouses. I had recently overheard my mother and Jenny in a shouting match about the sort of underwear my mother would and would not buy for a girl who'd just turned fourteen that October. 'Those are not for you. Those are for women,' my mother had said, looking into a catalogue Jenny was holding open. That was the first and maybe only time I heard Jenny shout, tears welling in her eyes, 'I am a woman!' after which she thundered down the hallway and hid away for hours in her room. Jenny's tantrum meant nothing to me. She'd always been the sort of kid who threw fits and slammed doors. But that she had ever considered herself a woman was news to me. I knew that I did not consider myself a man, especially during that interminably long first February in Salt Lake. I was a kid with a sore as hell arm in a sling and no friends, save for a dog I loved fiercely despite his funny name. The last place I wanted to be on a Friday afternoon was in the bleachers in the Billmore gymnasium watching hordes of girls, among them my sister, dance to the happy, echoing rhythm of 'Material Girl' as the Billmorette drill captains, Sara Chapman, Lisa Abraham, and a girl with whom

Jenny had somehow become friends, Janet Spencer, walked through the rows of dancers and tapped the shoulders of the clumsy and homely ones – you could see who they were a mile away because their hair fell over their faces, they tripped, they stepped out of line and off beat, and they seemed to hate themselves for every mistake they made – until only a handful of tall, coordinated, beautiful girls, whose entire bodies conformed to that loud, pulsating music, remained.

Jenny was one of those beautiful girls and she did not seem at all out of place. She wore a yellow T-shirt that said GIVE ME CHOCOLATE! and white tennis shorts, which my mother had bought a while ago at a secondhand shop, though they looked new and expensive as she danced next to other girls as tall and athletic and attractive as she. The girls were doing a shimmy with their hips, with their full torsos in fact, though the powerful motion of the hips swiveling, then grinding to a stop, then swiveling again, was what you noticed most. It was sexual. There was no other word for it, and Jenny was good, was adept at this. I had to wonder then how she had made friends and become talented in the same few weeks that I had been sitting around with my arm in a sling waiting for torn muscle and strained ligaments to heal. Only a few weeks before I'd been hurt, Mr. Bryant, the assistant basketball coach and health teacher, had asked me to try out for the junior varsity basketball team because I was tall. 'We need a boy with your height,' he'd said. Mr. Bryant didn't seem to doubt for a minute that I would make a good athlete, and I even began to picture myself leaping to the hoop and slamming one in, never mind the fact that I had never played the sport and that I couldn't jump more than an inch or two into the air. The cheerleaders would shake their pom-poms and scream for me. Even Tracy Bingham, the squad leader who drove a white Rabbit convertible and had perfect, medium-size breasts and a very nice smile, would notice me and begin to think about me sailing through the air with a basketball in my hand when she was trying to do her math homework at night. It was a silly fantasy, I knew, and I was ashamed of ever having dreamed it up, especially after my injury destroyed any remote chance that I might become a star athlete. It hardly mattered, I told myself. I had more important things than Tracy Bingham to think about. But somehow my sister was a success. She was an attractive teenage girl with social ambitions and friends, and I had no idea how she'd remade herself so quickly. Perhaps she'd been developing – growing taller, more beautiful, and popular – for a while, and I hadn't been looking. Sitting in those bleachers, I felt suddenly panicky. I felt suddenly that it was too late, though I wasn't sure exactly what was too late. Something had passed and I had missed it. That's all I knew.

Jenny made the team and as soon as the rejects had left the auditorium, the Billmorettes surrounded their new members and screamed and clapped and hugged them. They handed over to the new girls the red-and-gold Billmorette uniforms with the big *B* on the chest. I walked down the bleachers and faced my sister on the court, who made no sense to me as a Billmorette. 'Did you see? Did you see?' she shouted. When she tried to hug me, I let out a yelp and reminded her that my arm hurt, even though it hadn't hurt a bit when she'd grabbed me. I just felt that she should be cautious around my injury, that she should show some manners and consideration. But she was too damned excited to apologize.

'You have work to do at home,' I reminded her because someone had to lay down the law and insist she spend some time at the kitchen table trying to turn her C and C− grades into Bs. When we lived in Boise, she'd signed a contract with Mom that was taped on the refrigerator door and that said, 'I agree to get at least two Bs this term.' After breaking this contract, she was grounded to the house between the hours of three and five, her mandatory study time. But with both my parents working, I was the only one to enforce these study hours, which I did militantly because I understood how essential good study habits were. All the same, my father had given her permission to try out for the Billmorettes and do just about anything else she wanted to do when she wanted to do it.

'We have our first team meeting right now,' she said. 'Could you tell Mom to stop by school and pick me up on her way to get you at the hospital? Could you call her please and tell her that?' That afternoon was supposed to be my last appointment at The Richmond Clinics.

'I guess I could,' I said.

'Who's that?' Janet Spencer asked her.

'Oh,' Jenny said. It hadn't occurred to her until then that she was going to have to introduce me to her new friends. I didn't look so hot. I never did. Fashion was not a big concern of mine then. I wore a loose pair of Levis – another of my mother's great finds at Deseret Industries – that fell halfway down my butt and that I had to pull up fifty times a day. I pulled them up when Janet Spencer set her large blue eyes on me. My white, long-sleeved T-shirt said TEAM PLAYER on it for some reason. I hated wearing T-shirts with words on them, but more often than not the best secondhand clothes – the newest, most unused-looking clothes – were the ones with the silliest words on them. I had another that said SLED DOG on it, which was really a strange thing for a shirt to say. Of course, my arm was in a sling and I held my heavy backpack and red parka in my good hand. Janet Spencer wore the red-and-gold Billmorette uniform, the little skirt of which came up to the middle of her muscular thighs. Her hair was the blonde of lemon peel and her smile was incredibly white and large. She seemed to take me all in with that huge, terribly dishonest smile. 'This is my brother,' Jenny said.

'Cool,' Janet Spencer said.

'Nice to meet you,' I said.

'Yeah,' she said, turning away and plunging into a huddle of red-and-gold drill team girls. My sister waved a hand at me and said, 'See you in a couple hours'. I stood there for a while, alone in the middle of that court, holding my coat and heavy book bag and feeling how separate, how far away – a universe away – I felt from all those squealing girls who had just begun shouting out the first line of the Billmore fight song, which goes, '*Billmore! Billmore! Billmore is bold!*' I did that until my sister actually stuck her head out of the huddle and shouted silently – so that I could only see the word on her lips – 'Go, go, go'. So I did. I turned and headed for the main exit, which was all the way on the other side of that basketball court and seemed to take forever to reach.

It was a strange day for the end of February – rainy and muggy – and I spent the bus ride up to The Richmond Clinics watching beads of water flit across the window next to me. In the examination room, the doctor prodded at my shoulder and moved my arm in different angles before telling me that I'd healed up, that the strained ligaments and torn muscle were better than ever, and that there was no need to put the sling back on. He was a young guy with an absolutely bald head that shone orange and smooth in the light. 'You don't seem too happy about it,' he said. I said I was, even though I couldn't have felt less excited and I wanted to keep the sling, which he had been about to throw away. When I asked him if I could take it, he laughed and said, 'It's all yours'. Later, as I stood outside the entrance waiting for my mother to pick me up, my arm felt odd, skinny, naked without it. I stood just inside the awning, watching the rainwater run off the building. It put me in a trance – the water running down in strings and drumming against the sidewalk – so that I barely noticed the fact that I'd put the sling back on. My arm still hurt a little, or so it seemed to me, and I wondered if the doctor hadn't been wrong, if maybe my arm could use a few more days in that sling. Besides, I liked the way it felt and wanted to wear it a little while longer, the way you want to wear an old, holey T-shirt because the fabric is worn fine, nearly as comfortable as your own skin.

When I sat down in the car, my mother didn't say anything and didn't look over at me. She just pulled out of the parking lot and drove past the Fort Douglas Country Club and for some reason down the hill, which was the opposite direction we needed to be driving. She'd just gotten off work from Oak Groves and looked especially tired that day, her hair a little messed up where she'd worn the nurse's cap, a white hat that she'd thrown into the backseat of the Buick and that looked like one of those paper boats kids make in grade school. Jenny was sitting in the backseat, wearing her new Billmorette uniform. I guessed that my mother and she had been arguing since Jenny was quiet and quickly gave me a look of caution, a look that said something's wrong with Mom. When my mother looked over at me, I saw that her eyes were swollen and glossy red, that she'd been crying, and that something really was wrong. 'I thought they were letting you out of that thing today,' she said, gesturing at my sling.

'They asked me to wear it for another week or so,' I said, lying to avoid what I sensed was going to be a very unpleasant situation.

'Your arm is healing, isn't it?' she asked.

'I guess I'm not healing as well as they thought I would.'

'Why is that the case?' she asked.

'The doctors aren't sure.'

'Wonderful. Great,' my mother said. She looked at me, and I saw that she was not only sad but angry, too.

I should have stopped, but sometimes I just didn't know when to stop. 'They said it might take months more. They said they'd have to do some tests and things.'

'Jesus.' She hit the steering wheel with her hand. 'Why can't anything go right with this family? Why?'

'What's wrong with everybody?' I asked.

'Nothing,' my mother said. We'd stopped at a light, and she looked at me and smiled, as if to prove it. 'Nothing.' A tear dropped quickly from her eye, then another and another. She let out a laugh. 'Oh, shit,' she said.

'You're scaring me,' I said. I looked out my window at a hippie on a chopper who'd just pulled up beside us. He wore no helmet, and his long hair and beard dripped with rain. 'I want somebody to tell me what's wrong.'

'It's nothing. Nothing at all.' My mother put her head down on the steering wheel and really started to cry.

'The light's turned,' I said. The people behind us had begun honking. 'You have to go.' I nudged her, and she sat up and began driving, her eyes focusing, drying a little as she watched the road.

'Mr. Warner died today,' my mother said, looking

straight ahead. Mr. Warner, I guessed, was one of the tenants at Oak Groves. 'I have this job where people actually die, Steven. It's crazy, crazy. He just fell over on me. I couldn't believe his weight. I've never felt anything so heavy.'

'Who's Mr. Warner?' I asked.

'Just an old man,' she said. 'A very old man who died a few hours ago and fell on your mother. How insane is that?' She looked at me and began laughing out loud as the tears came to her eyes again. 'Now I have to go back there and talk to someone about it – the coroner or someone – so that they can make out a report. I'm the sole witness to Mr. Warner's death.' She was taking a left turn and stopped talking to concentrate on her driving before starting in again. 'I have to make a statement. I was telling him to lift his arms up so that I could sponge him there. That's when he fell on me. Jesus.' I could see by the way my mother was shaking her head back and forth, back and forth, that she was remembering it in detail and trying as hard as she could, flexing her jaw and then spitting out a laugh, not to remember it. In the backseat, Jenny was looking down at her lap. She'd probably heard the whole story by now. I could picture Jenny wanting to tell my mother about making the drill team, being a Billmorette, and then my mother telling her about the dead guy. 'He still had soap on him,' my mother continued, 'and I was rinsing him off. If you send them to lunch with soap suds still on them, they get sent back to you and you have to rinse them off again. That's when he just fell over on me like I was supposed to comfort him or do something. So now we need to go back there. I have to sign something. I guess that's what you do when somebody old with no living relatives dies. I didn't even know him. He was too old to know.'

'Are we going to Oak Groves right now?' I asked.

'He never said anything that made sense, anything that you could reply to,' she said. 'You can't get to know someone you can't have a conversation with, can you?'

She seemed to expect an answer from me, so I gave her one. 'Not really.'

'He just muttered all the time. A lot of the elderly at Oak Groves are like that. The other nurses tell me I'm going to get used to that. But I'm not used to it, and I don't want to get used to it. He couldn't hear you, either. When you'd say his name, you had to yell it right in his face as if you were calling to someone across a parking lot. It felt cruel. Even then he hardly knew to look at you. You can't get to know someone like that, can you?'

'I guess not,' I said.

She didn't say anything for a moment. 'I don't mean to be telling you all of this. But I haven't been able to talk to anybody yet.' She looked at her watch. 'It only happened a few hours ago. Afterwards, I took the others to lunch as if it were just any other day and none of it affected me at all. But it did. It really did. I don't think I can do this anymore.'

We drove through the intersection of 100 South and 200 East, exactly one block south and two blocks east of the Temple, I knew, because the grid system in Salt Lake was built around Temple Square. Every address told you where you were in relation to that silly-looking holy site. The City of Zion really was built around God. At a red light on Main Street, we stopped in front of the high stucco walls of Temple Square, behind which rose the Disney-like spires of the Temple itself with the golden statue of the Angel Moroni blowing a trumpet atop the highest central spire. Pedestrians hurried in and out of the Temple Square gates, huddled beneath umbrellas and newspapers and squinting into the wet air.

'When God returns,' Jenny said, 'the Angel Moroni will come to life and really blow his trumpet. That could happen at any time. It could happen now. That's when everybody will come back to life.' She was peering out the window at the angel and trying to distract us so that she wouldn't have to hear about Mr. Warner anymore. I saw her plan and I didn't want to hear any more about the old man, either, but I didn't much like what Jenny was saying. I didn't like having to picture, as I did then, everyone digging free of their graves and walking around in the afternoon sun, trailing black earth behind them, as golden Moroni blasted at his trumpet.

'Who told you that?' I asked, knowing what the answer would be.

'Janet Spencer,' she said. Janet Spencer was Mormon, as all the popular girls at Billmore were. She just happened to live up the street from us and wore the sort of trendy clothes that Jenny had to have ever since they had become friends. After school, Jenny spent hours over at Janet's place, where she had been learning not only what sort of clothes she should be wearing, but also what she should believe. On the last two Sundays, the Spencers had picked up Jenny in their Mercedes station wagon and driven her down the hill to their ward, where she prayed and read from the Bible and did whatever else Mormons do for the better part of the day. When our father questioned her, she said she didn't really believe in God or Mormonism. 'I look forward to it. I'm meeting people, and I like it,' she said. But on those two Sundays she had come back happy, humming and singing songs I'd never heard. And the fact that Janet Spencer had been brainwashing my sister with Mormon renditions of the end of the world worried me. Despite her denials, Jenny tended to believe things. She wanted to believe things. She should have been spending her time after school and on Sundays learning geometry and not hokey stories about Kingdom Come.

'Don't believe everything Janet Spencer says,' I said.

'I don't believe *everything*,' she said. All the same, she couldn't shut up about it. 'She taught me the Ten Commandments. Would you like to hear the Ten Commandments?'

'Not right now,' my mother said. 'I'm going to ask you two to please be quiet until we get to Oak Groves.'

The rain was coming down heavily now, beating against the hood and running down the windshield so fast that the wipers hardly made a difference. Then the rain, even as we sat at the light, eased up. I could see the reflection of my mother's face in the windshield, the wipers moving through it and the water flowing over it – her eyes, her nose, her mouth – but not changing it. 'I'd rather not go to that place,' I said. 'Maybe you could take Jenny and me home first.'

My mother glared at me and I could tell that, in that instant, she was furious with me. 'You're your father's son,' she said. 'You are. God help me.' The anger settled and steadied her and she drove now with a frightening ease and control. It was as if she had a goal, a purpose, and her anger had put her in mind of this fact.

'My shoulder hurts,' I said. 'The doctor said it might not heal for months. He said he didn't understand what was wrong with me.'

She looked over at me, though I didn't see concern in her eyes. I saw exhaustion and frustration and suspicion. She didn't believe me. 'Are you trying to add worry to my life? Is that what you're trying to do?' She took out a cigarette and lit it, seeming to draw more calm, more strength, as she inhaled and let out smoke. 'Somebody has to work in this family. Don't you two know that?'

'I know it,' Jenny said.

'You know why I'm working at this place, don't you? You know why I'm cleaning up after old people – mopping their urine off the floor, feeding them, watching them die.' She shook her head, then took a long draw from her cigarette.

'Jenny says she knows it,' I said.

'This is a question for you, Steven. I want you to think

about it now and I want you to give me an answer. I was just asking you to come along with me, to keep me company while I do this thing. That's all I wanted from you.' She let out a long, tired breath. 'This family,' she said.

'What's wrong with you?' I asked. 'You're acting strange.' I was angry or scared, I didn't know which. I only knew I had to fight her now, to resist something that I could sense was happening.

'What's wrong with me,' she said, 'is that I'm tired of carrying all the weight around here.' She was pulling into the parking lot of a Dee's Family Restaurant somewhere around Fourth. It wasn't the nicest restaurant, close enough to the park benches of the Town Hall and the warm, quiet shelter of the City Library to bring in the homeless, who were literally streaming through the doors as we pulled up. I was noticing how dirty the rain seemed, how it flooded the street gutters with a thick brown water and plastered discarded newspaper to the sidewalks and made the sky a blurry, concrete gray that seemed to absorb all distance and space. It was supposed to be winter, and I wished for the hard, bleak, leveling whiteness of snow, the quiet and sure way it lays itself down, erases things until the whole world is mute and soft and simplified.

'What are we doing here?' I asked.

'We're going to have a talk, Steven. There's no need to make this any more difficult than it needs to be. I don't mean to get angry at you. None of this is your fault, is it?' she said. I could tell she was trying to calm down, and I was glad. 'I thought I'd offer you a treat or something. How's that sound?'

'Why?' Jenny asked. She didn't understand any better than I did what entitled us to a treat.

'Because we need to talk about something,' my mother said.

I didn't like the sound of this at all. 'I thought we needed to go to Oak Groves now,' I said, an idea that suddenly seemed preferable to any talk. 'What about Mr. Warner?'

'Mr. Warner,' she said. She took a deep breath and seemed about to cry again. But then she put her hands squarely on her knees and looked out the windshield. 'Mr. Warner is dead,' she said. 'I guess he can wait for us.'

Standing just inside the door with menus in her hand, the hostess took one look at us – a woman and two kids – and said, 'Nonsmoking?' to which my mother shook her head and requested smoking, despite the fact that she had been attempting with some success to quit since we'd come to Salt Lake and that that particular section was overrun with all the bums trying to get out of the rain, drinking coffee and blowing cigarette smoke so thick a haze of gray hung in the air. We sat at a booth next to a rain-streaked window. Jenny said she was hungry in a very pleasant voice, though she was looking to the right of us where a bum and his girlfriend sat together. The bum wore two plastic bags cinched with rubber bands over his feet – one of which said GAP on it, a detail I hoped my sister hadn't missed. In the chair next to him, he had set a huge garbage bag of empty Coke cans that would probably purchase his lunch, or something else, later in the day. There were other bums in that place, too, a few in the booth in front of us and some at tables farther away from us; and I noticed then that beneath the heavy odors in that restaurant, odors of cigarette smoke and bacon and fried potatoes, lay another odor – the damp smell of animals – though it was not really a stink or even an unpleasant smell. It was just the smell of wet bodies warming up, drying off, the smell of Noir, for example, when he came in from the rain, the smell of the outdoors when it gets cramped up inside. I knew that the smell had been carried in by the people around us, and it made me feel a little unsafe and put me in mind of something that had happened a long time ago with my father, who had never had a lot of patience with these sorts of people. His take on bums was simple: They don't work. They sit around and expect something for nothing. You don't get something for nothing. Seeing a panhandler could set him off. 'You know something?' he'd say to them. 'I work. I get up every day and I go to work.' That was funny for him to say, since it was rarely true and was definitely not true during our time in Salt Lake when he worked three times a week at the garage and went to school the other two days.

The thing that happened had to do with this very nice pair of shoes. We were living in Boise at the time and my father had just had a heated face-to-face with someone at the phone company about his choice not to pay for a feature on our service that we had never ordered and had never used. He had been arguing with a woman supervisor who kept repeating the same line to him. 'I'm sorry, sir. I wish I could help you. But our policy is not my policy. It is the company's policy.' His voice kept getting louder while hers remained at the same dispassionate, monotonous tone. It drove him mad. I don't remember whether he'd won or lost that argument, though my father did not often carry his side of arguments. After leaving the phone company, we ran into the man with the shoes sitting outside against a brick wall and holding up a sign that said MONEY FOR FOOD. My father stood over him and said nothing. An elderly woman stepped around him to drop a few coins into the man's cup. She gave my father an odd look as she walked down the sidewalk, but he did not move. He just stood there until the man looked up and said, 'You going to give me money or not?'

'Excuse me,' my father said, and the beggar repeated his question. 'No way in hell,' my father said. 'Not when you wear shoes like that.' The man's shoes were black leather, shiny, unmarked, and obviously new. They fastened in the front with a silver buckle. 'Your shoes are nicer than mine, and you're asking me for money. No,' he said again. 'No way in hell.' It was true that the shoes were very nice despite the fact that the man's other clothes – his ragged blue jeans and dirty white T-shirt – were what you might have expected from a beggar. The man's face was dirty and skinny. His lips were swollen and his lower lip was chapped and split in the middle. His beautiful black shoes, however, were a mystery. My father pointed down at his own shoes then, an old pair of blue Adidas, one of them with a gash in the side so large that you could see part of my father's socked foot. 'Look at my shoes, for Christ's sake.' He was too angry, and it worried me. The fact was, my father had nicer shoes at home in his closet, a pair of dress shoes and maybe some house slippers, all of them nice enough, even if they were not quite as new-looking as this stranger's shiny black leather shoes with silver buckles. The beggar's shoes certainly were not my father's style, since the buckles gave them a boyish appearance. All the same, they had really set him off. My father turned and pointed at me, at my shoes. 'Look at my son's shoes.' My shoes were white sneakers, though the white had worn to a dirty brown, and I could remember finding them at a secondhand shop in very good shape; I could remember how excited my mother had been that they fit me since my foot was unusually narrow and we so often had to settle for shoes that my feet swam in. Now they were old, it was true. But once they'd been very good shoes, and we'd been lucky to find them. I wished he hadn't pointed to me. 'You think I am going to give you money when I can't afford better shoes for my son? Is that what you think?'

My father took a step closer to the man, who stood up then, I think, to protect himself. 'Stop pointing at my shoes,' the man said, which was strange since my father had been pointing at our shoes.

'I'd like to know where you got them,' my father said. 'That's what I'd like to know.'

'You can go to hell,' the beggar said.

'You're asking us for money!' my father shouted.

'This is harassment. He's harassing me!' the man shouted into the street. But the sidewalks were mostly empty and a few passers-by on the other side of the street decided to ignore the situation.

'I want to know where you got those,' my father said.

'You can fuck off!' the man shouted.

'You're asking us for money!' my father shouted again. He walked right up to the beggar and pushed him once. He sort of hit him with both hands out flat on the chest, shoved him away, and caused the plastic foam cup the man had been holding to fall and spill coins over the sidewalk.

The beggar didn't look once at the money. You could see his skinny, dry face fill with rage. 'You don't touch me! Don't you dare touch me!' My father took one and then another step back. He grabbed my arm, and we started walking fast for the car as the beggar, still furious, followed us. I remember his thick, sweet garbage smell very close behind us and the broken, raw anger in his voice. 'You touch me again, I'll have you and your son locked up, you hear? You hear?' My father opened the car door for me and got in on his side as the beggar kept yelling, 'You hear? You hear?' He kept shouting at us even as we drove away. I watched him shake his arms in the air behind us and then disappear as we turned the corner.

When we stopped at the first light, my father hit the steering wheel with his fist about a half dozen times. 'Did you see that guy's shoes? Jesus.' I didn't know what to say. I had been terrified that something bad had been about to happen between my father and the other man, that they would hit each other, that someone would get hurt. For the rest of the drive home, my father was preoccupied. He turned the radio on. He searched for a station – country, rock, classical – but nothing seemed to sound right to him, and he switched it off. He rifled in the glove box for a cassette tape he couldn't find and swore and swerved out of his lane. He kept whispering something to himself, and once he even pulled off the road and into a parking lot and looked over at me. 'I've got to ask you something,' he said. I nodded. 'Do you believe that we are going to be doing better someday? Do you believe me when I say that we are going to buy ourselves a house in a few years and move in for good?'

'Sure,' I said.

'A house with a nice yard and separate rooms for you and Jenny, a room for your mother and me, and a nice front room and kitchen. You believe we're going to get that someday?' In those days, the house we talked about was more modest, more our size. It wasn't until later, after my father had failed again and again to establish himself in a job, that we somehow began talking about a three-story house with large windows and five bathrooms and a swimming pool.

'Yes,' I said. 'I always believed that.'

That seemed to help him, and he was able to pull himself together and get back on the road. But closer to home, when we stopped at another light, he hit the wheel with the palm of his hand again and said, in a fierce whisper, 'Those goddamned shoes'. I wanted him to forget about the shoes, but I saw in his face as he looked at the road that he couldn't.

If you don't want to talk to someone, you don't look at them. My little sister evidently hadn't learned that yet because she was staring right at the bum next to us. She was a beginner when it came to interacting with strangers. She still thought everybody in the world was more or less safe. It was hard not to look at him, though, with his feet covered nearly to the knee in plastic bags. Jenny stared right at the Gap bag, and the bum seized the moment, lifting that leg up and winking at her. 'How do you like my galoshes?' he asked.

She looked away, pretending he wasn't there, and put her napkin in her lap. 'At Janet Spencer's house,' she said, 'they always put their napkins in their laps as soon as they sit at the table. Then they say grace. They fold their arms like this.' She folded her arms.

'We're not saying grace,' I said.

'They work, believe it or not,' the woman who sat opposite the bum said. The woman was extremely thin, especially in the face, where you could see the bony round shape of her eye sockets. She wore this fake fur that was matted down with water.

'I'm sure they do,' my mother said, smiling and pretending to admire the bum's weird footwear.

'You have to improvise sometimes,' the man said. 'You have to be handy and work with what you've got.'

'It looks like you do just fine for yourself,' my mother said. I didn't know why she had to speak to them. They didn't look dangerous, but they were dirty and wet and had that smell of the outdoors on them. What struck me most about the woman was the fact that she had once been beautiful. Her face was too thin now and she was soaked, her wet, shoulder-length hair black as ink and stuck together in strands. But you could see the places in her face where the beauty had worn down and left her bony and tired in the eyes.

'I'm not going to tell you a story about a bus ticket I need to buy,' the man said. 'This is my entire story.' He hit the bag of aluminum cans. 'Instead, I'm just going to ask if you might have a little money to spare. Five dollars, maybe?' He looked at me and winked. I was astonished, then angry. That was a hell of a lot to ask for. We did not have five dollars to give away.

'Maxwell is trying the direct approach on my advice,' his girlfriend, or whoever she was, said. 'Just tell them what you want. People don't like to be lied to. It's a matter of mutual respect.'

My mother was fishing through her purse. 'We don't have any money to give you,' I said. But she suddenly had three dollars in her hand for him.

'No,' I said. The bum had his hand ready to grab for the

money, but he held it back then, as if afraid something might bite him.

'Don't you tell me no,' my mother said.

'We can't afford this.'

My mother leveled her eyes at me. 'I determine that. You got it?' I nodded, though I couldn't believe it. More than any of us, my mother understood that our family had certain limits, that we had to be careful, that we'd be lucky just to get what we needed. Besides, she had never been an especially charitable person. She'd always been defensive and careful with money.

'Kids,' the bum said, taking her money. I hated him. 'Thank you very much.' Then he winked at her cigarettes on the table and said, 'And maybe two or three of those for later.' That was funny because his girlfriend had been smoking non-stop since we sat down. All the same, my mother gave them three cigarettes. I didn't get it.

'Honesty is the best policy,' his girlfriend said. 'Just ask for what you want. Don't make up stories. Am I right?'

They stood up, seeming to realize that it was time for them to go. The man removed an invisible hat from his head and tipped it at my mother. I didn't understand why they left then since it was still raining hard, and I watched them walk into the storm, the enormous load of aluminum cans on the man's back and the odd plastic bags fastened to his feet. They weren't hurrying, just walking in the downpour the way only people who have nowhere to go must be used to doing. It depressed me, watching them like that, though I still thought we'd been crazy to give them what we needed for ourselves, which my mother must have seen on my face when I turned around and looked at her again.

'I make the decisions,' she said. 'Okay?'

'Okay,' I said.

It turned out that our charity cases were criminals, since they'd left without paying for their coffees. The waitress had a stand-off over their abandoned table with her manager, a young guy with a soft, fat Mormon face and a skinny body, who shook his head at her, dug into his lardy cheek with his thumb and forefinger because it hurt him to say, though he kept saying it anyway, 'Someone has to pay for this. It's your job to keep an eye on your tables.' This incident made me feel good; it showed that at fifteen I had sound judgment.

Our waitress – the one who had been stiffed by Maxwell and his girlfriend – was a plump woman whose chin sunk into her loose neck. Her name tag said SANDY. 'We're sorry about your table,' my mother said.

'What happened to you, honey?' the waitress asked me. I didn't know what she meant at first. Then I remembered that my arm was still in a sling, and I felt what I'd felt over the last few weeks when people asked me about it – appreciative and self-conscious. I liked people to notice. It always surprised me how many strangers actually cared about what happened to people they didn't know.

'Just an accident,' I said.

'It's a good thing your mother's a nurse,' Sandy said,

noticing my mother's all-white Oak Groves uniform. Then she read my T-shirt out loud. 'Team Player. You must be on the basketball team. That how you hurt your arm?' People always thought I was a basketball player because of my height.

'No.' I hated it when I had to tell people I didn't play the sport, especially after Mr. Bryant had asked me to try out for the team. It made me feel like a failure at something I had never done.

'She must do something, though,' Sandy said, gesturing at Jenny's uniform.

'I'm on the drill team,' Jenny said.

My mother smiled. 'My son is always getting hurt,' she said. I guessed she'd said that just to be pleasant and conversational, since it was hardly true. I was a cautious, unathletic kid who almost never got hurt. In my free time, I did things like read – mostly science fiction novels. I liked to sit around and think about the possibility of other planets out there being populated by intelligent life. That was one of my favorite thoughts, even though it seemed unlikely, even though I was more or less convinced that the earth was the only minuscule spot of life in all of space and time. It was nice to think that we were not entirely alone. I also liked to build models – mostly of war planes from World War II – though they were expensive, and at fifteen I was getting too old for that sort of thing. I thought a lot about war, whether I would or would not be afraid, what it would be like to kill or be killed. I thought about being a pilot, about flying, about doing that despite the fact that my vision was imperfect. (My mother would often remind me that military pilots needed to have perfect eyesight.) I wanted to see the earth, America, Salt Lake City, the Downs, my street, our little duplex from the sky, where everything, lakes and mountains, seemed tiny and insignificant and under your power. Otherwise, I did not have a lot of interests. If I didn't have my face in a book, I was watching TV. My favorite programs other than sci-fi shows were the nature documentaries about the struggles of the insect world, about microbes and bacteria, about the carnivores of Africa. That was drama, and the fact that that sort of struggle was not fictionalized, was real, gave me a charge even though I was anything but a carnivore of Africa, even though I was this pale ecto-morph with straight black hair that, no matter how often I washed it, was always a little greasy and lay flat on my head. I wasn't the most handsome kid, especially in contrast to my sister and mother, who were beauties. Later, I would become better-looking. But at that time, I was in an ugly phase. The fine wire rims and oval lenses of my new eyeglasses gave me a sophisticated, intellectual look that I'd never had before. But that wasn't quite enough. With my shirt off I was all bones, sternum, ribs, and clavicles. A triangular patch of acne above my nose flared up weekly, bloody and conspicuous because I couldn't stop myself from bothering it, picking at it. I was awkward, avoided social situations, and probably hated myself a little more than the average teenager. The fact that I'd stood up to Danny Olsen and fought him was less

the most expensive items on the menu. 'You won't even like that,' I said. 'It's seafood.'

'I like seafood,' she said.

'You don't know what seafood is.'

'I do, and I like it.'

'Don't let her order that,' I told my mother.

'Jenny can make her own decisions,' she said.

'Jesus. I don't understand this. I don't understand why you're letting things get so crazy.'

My mother didn't even look at me. She just informed Sandy that we were in a rush and that she'd tip generously if Sandy could make it quick. 'There,' she said once Sandy had gone. 'It's nice to see that you two are hungry.' She lit a cigarette, and I could see that the hand that she held the cigarette with was trembling a little, just barely, that she was still frightened or shaken up and hiding it pretty well. 'Do you have your answer yet, Steven?' she asked.

'My answer to what?'

'You were supposed to be thinking about something.' I knew what she meant, but I didn't let on. 'About why I work at Oak Groves. About why I had to hold a dead man in my arms today.' She waited for my response. 'Well?'

'I'm still thinking.'

'I know,' Jenny said.

'This is between your brother and me.'

I had to sit there and ponder that question because in all honesty I didn't know the answer or why she was even asking the question. 'I'm still thinking,' I said, because she was giving me this cold stare. Sandy had already brought our waters by that time, and I had begun to notice something very strange and more than a little unsettling. Over the speakers a very soft choral version of 'Joy to the World' was playing despite the fact that Christmas had happened two months ago. That seemed wrong – Christmas music out of season. It gave me that feeling of something having passed, something out of reach and gone, the same feeling I got every year when I saw people dragging their trees out to the curb to be picked up for trash. All those dead trees lying on the curbs of a whole city – that was a depressing thing to see. They shouldn't have been playing Christmas music, not in February. 'I'm thinking. I'm thinking,' I said.

'I'll give you the answer. The answer to why I work at Oak Groves is that I love you. That's the answer, Steven,' she said, though in a not particularly loving way.

'I love you, too,' I said in a not particularly loving way.

'I do it because I love you,' she said again, maybe because she was trying to convince me of it this time. But all I heard was her nerves, her shaky voice.

'I love you, too,' Jenny said in her frightened little girl's voice. At that moment, I hated the way she reverted to being a kid. I wanted to hit her. Against whatever was happening that afternoon, I was pretty sure that fear and smallness would not help us.

'This is between Mom and me,' I said to her.

'I do it because I want you to have food on the table. I do it because I want you to have insurance. I want you to be safe.'

'Thank you,' I said.

We stared at each other then for a long time, my mother smoking down her cigarette and lighting another while Jenny drew hearts with her index finger in the steamy window next to us. 'Does anyone want to hear the Ten Commandments now?' my sister asked.

'No,' I said.

'I'd like to say them. I really would.'

'Later, sweetie,' my mother said to her.

The food came then – the burger, two open buns with cheese melted over the beef patties on one bun and a stack of lettuce, onion, and tomato on the other bun. The portion of onion rings was enormous, taking up the rest of the plate. I wasn't used to restaurant food – the amounts, the display – and it did seem to me as if unexpected riches sat before me, though those were not the sentiments I tried to convey when I said, 'And here's the food on the table.'

'You're not going to make this easy for me, are you, Steven?'

'What easy?' I asked. 'What's happening? What are you trying to do?'

She put her purse on the table and took a letter from it. 'I want you to see something,' she said, handing me the letter. It was addressed to my father – Mr. William Parker – at our address. I took the letter out and saw that it was his report card from Salt Lake Community College. Jenny scooted over toward me, and we both read.

Federal Taxation I	D
Management Accounting	F
Financial Accounting II	F

It was report card season, and Jenny and I had both brought ours home a month before. I'd done well as usual, receiving all As with the exception of one B+ in shop, a class that I loathed. Even Jenny, with her C– average, had done better than our father. 'He flunked out,' I said.

'He could try again,' Jenny said.

'Not for three thousand dollars, he can't. That's what it cost us for him to flunk out. He's worse than your sister,' my mother said. 'Maybe we need to ground him to the house and let you loose on him, Steven.'

'That's not funny,' I said. 'Maybe he *could* try again. Maybe we could use the money from my arm. Couldn't we do that?'

My mother laughed. 'It wasn't that much money, Steven. Not enough, anyway, to keep it from disappearing as soon as your father got his hands on it.'

'It's gone?' I asked. I really had thought it was more. I'd thought it was enough to keep us secure for a while, a year or two, until my father got out of school and he could begin earning a real salary.

She nodded her head.

'He could try again anyway,' I said. 'Times are good, aren't they?' She didn't say anything. 'Why are you showing me this?' I gave the report card back to my mother. I didn't want to have to look at it anymore.

'I want you to know my reasons, I guess. You're smart, Steven. You know we can't stay with him.'

'*We*,' I said. 'Don't say *we*!'

Jenny sat back in her seat now, her face going blank. She was getting the drift of this expensive, indulgent meal. She had already torn into her plate of fried fish and had managed to eat only bits of it. 'It's all fish,' she said. 'I guess I don't like fish.' Then she put her hands to her ears, the way she did whenever she didn't want to hear something, and said, 'I don't want to talk about this anymore.' She got up then and left the table.

'Don't you say *we*,' I said again. Then I picked up my burger and began to eat it ravenously, bite after bite, the edges of the bun dripping with the white-and-red flow of ketchup and mayonnaise, lettuce and onions spilling out onto the plate.

'Slow down,' my mother said. 'You're going to choke yourself.'

My eyes were watering from stuffing too much food in my mouth. I drank half my glass of ice water. My chin was dripping with condiments. 'He got one D-,' I said through the food in my mouth. I put my index finger up. 'He passed one class, didn't he? So he's not a good student. So what?'

'Please wipe your mouth,' my mother said. I picked up the other half of my burger and began to devour it, my cheeks bulging with meat and bread. 'I'm not going to watch this,' she said. I had this thought then that I was like a carnivore of Africa, that I was a cat or jackal who tore and ripped chunks of food from still-struggling prey. It was a stupid thought, but it made me feel powerful and capable of anything I might need to do to get what I wanted. She looked away. I began to inhale the onion rings, one after another, crumbs falling to the plate until my mouth was so dry I could no longer chew without drinking water. I finished my water, reached across the table, picked up my mother's water, and started in on that. I just kept thinking that I was a carnivore, that nothing could get in the way of my appetite. Nothing.

'There,' I said when I was done, 'you can look now.'

She looked. 'Are you going to wipe your mouth?'

'No.' I could feel the food dripping down my chin. She reached over and took a swipe at me with her napkin, but missed.

'Please,' she said. 'Would you please wipe your mouth?'

I didn't. I just sat there, looking and feeling like an animal, wanting to believe that this was just another one of those times when she'd threaten to leave and finally wouldn't. But something about the way she held herself, the way she was very much in control now, told me that this time was different. She actually wiped her own clean mouth with her napkin, as if that would take care of the food dripping down mine.

Jenny came back then, one hand still over an ear and the other holding one of those paper place mats kids color on and a small box of broken crayons. She sat down and began coloring in this farmyard scene with a farmhouse and a fenced-in yard with all of Old MacDonald's animals – pigs and chickens, cows, sheep, and dogs and cats – thrown in together, craning their heads out between rungs of this fence and goggling their animal eyes at you. Jenny had always been a neat-as-hell colorer, producing polished, little-kid coloring masterpieces with not a molecule of crayon outside the lines. In the past, whenever we'd had the money to eat out, she'd win restaurant coloring contests and get plenty of praise from my father for all the free meals her pictures earned over the years. It used to make me jealous. But it was just coloring. It wasn't oil painting. It wasn't even drawing. It was a knack for laying it on evenly and for observing boundaries, not crossing lines. She didn't say anything. She was in her zombie zone, where the rest of the world disappeared and where she went a lot of the time when she was upset. It was either the zombie zone or a total, all-out tantrum when Jenny got upset. She had chosen the zone, and now I had to deal with the shit while she colored. 'Great,' I said. 'That's very pretty, Jenny.' Of course, she just kept coloring.

I looked back at my mother and asked her the same questions my father asked her whenever she threatened to leave. 'Where are you planning to go? You don't have any money. You don't know anyone in Salt Lake.'

'Don't you dare play that game with me, Steven.' She pointed at me with her book of matches. 'Anyway, I have a job. I can take care of myself. I can take care of us.'

'Where?' I asked. 'I just want to know where you'll go.'

'Okay,' she said, 'I'm just going to say it.'

'Say what?'

'I'm just going to say it.'

'Then say it.'

She hesitated, lit another cigarette, crossed and re-crossed her legs beneath the table. 'Jenny, you should listen, too, okay?' But Jenny was all artist. She was bent over her masterpiece and determined not to let the world interfere with her work. I had to admit, she was doing good work. I mean, she was definitely overachieving. She'd already laid out a plush layer of grass in a Crayola green so vividly and evenly applied that you almost believed in that grass. Now she was doing the fence in a brown that somehow teased out the rough, uneven graininess in real wood. The only thing that bothered me was those animals – the way they had all been thrown in the same enclosure together. You obviously don't do that with animals. Of course, it wasn't the purpose of that sort of picture to teach common sense. Still, it seemed like something a three-year-old should know: you don't put the cat in with the chickens.

'Steven,' I heard my mother's voice say, 'please look at me.' I was stuck in that farmyard full of happy, stupid animals who should have been tearing each other apart and weren't. 'Steven,' she said again. I looked at her. 'I have someone else,' she said in this very calm, soft voice.

The music over the intercom then was 'Silent Night' played by violins. Someone somewhere asked a waitress why they had to be playing Christmas music, and I heard her say, very distinctly, 'It's the only music we have, I'm afraid.'

'What?' I said to my mother. But she wasn't looking at me anymore. She was looking out the window. I wanted more food, but my plate was empty. I'd even eaten the quarter-slice of dill pickle and the piece of parsley garnish. There was nothing left. I just wanted to bite into something, so I grabbed a chunk of fried fish from Jenny's plate – a crab claw or something – and had to spit it out into my hand because I hated the weird ocean-stink taste of seafood.

'Here,' my mother said, quickly swooping it up with a clean napkin and rolling it into a neat, white ball that she placed back on Jenny's plate. She knew how to make anything look good. She really did.

'Someone else what?' I felt something happening to me, tears maybe. They just came in a rush and fell over my clean plate, red from the ketchup on my chin as if I were bleeding. I didn't know why her voice had to be so calm, so even and sure when she'd said that.

'He's serious about me.' She wasn't looking at me. She was looking at the haze of smoke she'd just blown into the air where she seemed to have fixed her eyes on some very complicated and painful thought. 'He's serious about *us*,' she said.

'He doesn't even know *us*,' I half shouted. I wanted to bark or growl or yell. But instead an odd thought came to me. 'Isn't that illegal? Can't Dad make you stay with us?'

'Isn't what illegal?' she said.

'Fucking someone else when you're married. Isn't that illegal? Haven't you been fucking him?'

'You watch your mouth, mister,' she said. She reached across the table and snatched the wrist of my good hand and squeezed it in her grip with surprising strength, until my bones started to hurt. 'I'm not going to stand for accusations like that,' she said. She let my hand go and pointed her cigarette at my forehead. 'You wipe your mouth. Right now. Wipe it!' I obeyed her. Sandy came then with my hot-fudge sundae. She must have sensed something because she quickly put the sundae down in front of me and took away the plate with my red tears on it. 'Please eat your dessert like a civilized person,' my mother said. When she saw that I was going to obey her, she said, 'I'm sorry, Steven. I shouldn't have grabbed you like that. This thing isn't easy for any of us.' She looked out the window again where the rain came down steadily and the heavy traffic on Main rushed by, spraying water from the gutters onto the sidewalk. 'I wish you would listen to me, Jenny,' she said. Jenny was changing crayons and eyeing the variety of animals over which she was laboring now. 'All right, fine,' my mother said. 'I'm going to talk and hope that maybe you're hearing me. Good enough.' She looked at her cigarettes and seemed to be counting them; then she looked at me. 'His name is Curtis Smith. He's a lawyer, divorced. He works very hard and has a couple of kids a little younger than you and Jenny. They live between his house in the Avenues and his ex-wife's house. I know him because his mother stays at Oak Groves. He treats her very well, visits her almost every day, makes sure she has fresh flowers in her room, that she's taken care of. That's important, you know, the way a man treats his family.'

'So you've only known him for a month?' I knew this must be true since she'd started working at Oak Groves within the last month. 'That's not long enough to know anything,' I said. 'Even I know that.'

'That's my business, not yours, Steven.' I could see, however, that this fact bothered her. 'Curtis loves me,' she said. 'I know that. He comes to Oak Groves almost every day. You can tell when a person is honest with you and when a person isn't. He's honest. I know that, too.'

'Do you love him?' I asked. Jenny lifted her picture into the air and looked at it. She was trying to gauge something – what color to use, how thickly to apply it, maybe. The thing that got to me was that she was crying – her face running with tears – only silently and in a way that wasn't interfering with her work, because she was still doing an amazing job with that picture. It made my throat catch, seeing Jenny like that. When she'd cry, she'd bawl and scream and snot up and shriek. I'd never seen her cry quietly, to herself, the way adults cry. I pushed my half-eaten sundae away. It was too much – too sweet, too heavy – and my stomach began to ache.

My mother was looking at her hand with the cigarette in it. I noticed that it was not trembling anymore. It was steady. She knew very well that Jenny had lost it, but she wasn't going to let that get in her way. 'I know enough about him to know that my reasons for wanting to be with him are good ones,' she said. 'I know that.'

'Dad loves you,' I said. 'Dad loves you more than anyone.'

'Maybe he does,' she said. 'But he's like a child that way. It's too much, and it's the wrong kind of love.' She looked down at her cigarette in the ashtray. 'I think your father needs me. I don't think he really loves me. If he loved me, he wouldn't keep doing this to me.' She tapped his report card with her fingers.

'That's not true,' I said. 'You know that's not true.' She couldn't contradict me this time because both of us knew how absolute and irrefutable the fact of his love for her was. He loved her desperately. He always had. 'I love you,' I said. 'But if you do this, I'll stop loving you. I promise I will.'

She smiled at me and let out a tired-sounding laugh. 'This isn't about you,' she said. 'Really, it isn't.' She put out a hand to touch my face, but I pushed it away. 'Okay,' she said. 'I understand.'

'Don't say that,' I said.

'I want you to understand,' she said. 'I want both of you to understand. I'm running out of time. I can't take care of your father forever. I'm still reasonably pretty. I'm young enough to do this, and I might not be next year. I guess I can't expect you to understand that, can I? I guess that's too much to ask.'

I looked at her then and saw her perhaps the way a man

would see her. My mother was a pretty woman, beautiful even, thin and tall with a narrow face and shoulder-length blonde hair. She had a scar on her left cheek — a dash of tender white flesh — from falling on the ice as a little girl. Her breasts were larger than average, as far as I knew, though not something you noticed right away about her. She had nice posture, and people, strangers, often complimented her on that, asked if she was a dancer. Her parents, both dead, had been proud people and had taught her how to carry herself accordingly, she'd told me. She had a small waist, which she claimed the cigarettes helped her keep. She might have been thirty-five or thirty-six that first year in Salt Lake; she'd had me as a very young woman not long after my father and mother had met in Bozeman, where she'd dropped out of nursing school, against the will of her parents, to marry my father. I had seen her shake her head many times and ask me and herself out loud why she just hadn't waited a little longer, at least until she'd finished school. She must have been even more beautiful then, and I thought about my mother as a young woman, before she had been my mother, and how she had been willing to give up her education for my father, how they had met in the bar at the Grand Henry Hotel, where a piano player always performed jazz standards and where my mother sat with a girlfriend named Edith, who had also been pretty, but nothing compared to her, according to my father. My mother had been the only young woman in the early 1960s in Bozeman who wore her hair short. He bought Edith and my mother drinks would ask about his mother. I did not want to have to look across the table at my mother and see how in her all-white nurse's uniform with her name tag on her chest – MARY PARKER, it said – she looked clean and maybe even a little younger than she was. I'd always known she was a pretty woman. But that afternoon was the first time I saw how a man might want my mother, and it was not a very pleasant thing to see. That her life expanded beyond the boundaries of who she was to me and my family only angered me.

'If we went with Curtis,' she said, 'I could quit my job at Oak Groves. I could quit today.'

'Stop saying *we*,' I said.

She looked at me very hard. 'I'm sorry, Steven,' she said. 'But whether you like it or not, you're dependent on me. Your father can't take care of you. You know that.'

'Are you going to quit?' I asked.

'I don't know yet. I don't like taking care of sick people. The mess of it.' She was remembering Mr. Warner – the dead Mr. Warner – and started to freak a little again. 'I just end up hating them for being sick and old and needy. That's not fair to them, or to me. You understand that I'd go on doing this for you and Jenny. I'd watch a hundred Mr. Warners die. But I can't go on doing it for your father. Not for one minute more.

I smiled at her as nicely as I could. I knew what I was going to say next and I wanted it to work, to win her over. 'Then keep on doing it for Jenny and me. Just for now. Just a little while longer. Please.'

'Of course,' she said, smiling back and looking at me as if she understood what I wanted, as if she wanted it, too. She reached across the table and put her hand in my hair and tousled it. 'I would. I really would. But I'm running out of time, kiddo.' She took her hand away and picked up her cigarette. 'Curtis would like to meet you. He'd like to meet both of you this afternoon. He's looking forward to it.'

'No,' I said. 'No way.

She was looking down at her water, staring at it as if she were trying to make it boil. She hadn't seemed to hear me. 'We've just got to take this one step at a time. Right now, we'll go take care of Mr. Warner. We'll worry about the rest after that.'

That's when I felt all that food I'd shoveled in grumbling inside me, hot and acidic. My stomach turned and a sharp, building pain pulsed at the center of my gut. I had to go. It was urgent. 'Where are you off to, Steven?' my mother asked.

'To take a dump,' I said, loud enough for the other diners in the restaurant to hear. I didn't mind if I ruined everybody's appetites. What did it matter at that point what I said? I moved quickly past a family of three extremely blond little girls all dressed in the same pink overalls and strung in a line of clasped hands between their blond parents. They sang a song and the littlest one picked her feet up and hung above the floor as her bigger sisters carried her. God, did I have to hold it. It was a matter of intense focus and willpower, and when I got to the end of gradually, in the midst of that gorgeous humming, he did his business – a slow, watery letting go – while I sat locked in my stall, clenched up and unable to do mine and trying to hold on to his voice even as he shat next to me and added his own sharp, distinct smell to the already spoiled air of that rest room. I wanted to cry, then, perhaps because of the slow, obvious perfection of his voice, or perhaps because of the almost suffocating stink in the air. I didn't, though. I looked up and read a string of disgusting bits of graffiti. 'You're the log maker,' one read. 'Fuck, fuck, fuck,' another said. 'You fudge packing ass lover.' They were spiteful words, and as I read them the huge bum next door kept up his merciful humming and I listened, trying to find the shadowy bottom of his voice, trying to fall all the way to its dark floor, trying to break through to a place so deep that I could no longer rise up, a place so far away that I could never leave and go back out to that particular day, which was buried and forgotten now in the stink and beauty of that restroom. I just sat on the toilet and listened to him. When I heard the bum rip into the toilet paper, I fastened myself back up, watched myself slide along the strip of mirror above the sinks, and left the bathroom. It was bright and loud and too spacious out in the restaurant now, and I half wanted to return to the men's room. I made myself hurry back to our table, though I couldn't help asking myself if all the bums smoking in that restaurant and trying to keep out of the rain didn't have some secret gift, too, a great voice or an ability to dance or some other facility you'd never expect.

I thought for sure that someone somewhere would pay the man in the bathroom to hum – pay him money so that he wouldn't have to be homeless. I wondered if all grungy people everywhere didn't have something beautiful that they could do. I hoped so.

When I got back to our table, Jenny told me that our mother had left to pay the bill and make a phone call. She was gone long enough for the bum from the bathroom to sit down at the table next to us with a Mormon missionary, who ordered decaffeinated tea – he wouldn't pay for coffee – and toast for the bum. Another missionary sat a few tables away, ministering to a teenage girl whose long blond hair was stringy and soaked. Both missionaries wore suits and ties, and the one at the table next to ours had large pink ears and very short hair that was still beaded with water from the rain. He couldn't have been older than eighteen, and I was sure he knew nothing about his companion's amazing voice. The missionary was talking about how God spoke to him. 'Really?' the bum asked. 'You hear his voice? What's it like? Is it like a human voice?'

'Sure,' the missionary said.

'A man's or a woman's voice?' The bum seemed very interested.

'A man's,' the missionary said. When the toast and tea came, the missionary made them say a silent prayer and they bowed their heads and closed their eyes. The bum's thick fingers drummed slowly on the tabletop.

After the prayer, the bum opened his eyes. 'I didn't hear

any voice,' he said. In the bum's huge hands the slices of toast seemed as small as playing cards. He ate each slice in two or three bites, and then looked over at our table. 'Is anyone going to eat that?' he asked, pointing at Jenny's full plate of fish.

'It's not mine,' I said. I was wishing that our mother would return. I was wishing that people would stop asking us for things. It didn't much matter to me anymore whether he could hum or not. I just wanted to be left alone.

'To whom does it belong?' the bum said. He actually said that – '*to whom*' – with this very exact pronunciation. I pointed to Jenny, who was finished with her coloring and was now just looking at what she had done. 'That's splendid,' the bum said. 'Really. Your sister has something there.' She didn't know, of course, what I did – that this man was himself a kind of artist and that his opinion meant something. We all looked at her picture – the missionary, the singing bum, and me – and I think we all saw that it was a little remarkable – the perfection of each animal, the green of the grass, the brown of the fence, the golden circle of the sun in a sky that she had touched with blue and tinted with silver and somehow managed to give depth to. We all looked at her then, at her face, still red from tears. She was done crying, but you could see that she was still suffering.

'I didn't hear God's voice, either,' Jenny said. I guess she'd been praying along with them, and that upset me. I didn't know why she insisted on being religious.

'You have to keep an open heart,' the missionary said. The fact that he was just a few years older than me didn't stop him from pretending to be the only one of us to whom God spoke.

The bum pointed at her plate of fish. 'Go ahead,' she said. He ate rapidly and neatly, and I couldn't help feeling that I was tired of giving people things that day, even if they were things we didn't want and even if this guy was hungry and, as I knew, exceptional in his way. I could understand then why my father had yelled at the man with nice shoes. I could understand his feeling that we worked hard for the little we had, that feeling that anything could be taken away from you, that somebody else having something meant that you couldn't have it, that feeling – simple and immediate – that you could lose everything in an instant. I was pretty sure the bum would leave us alone now, though I was wrong about that. When my mother returned, she left a four-dollar tip on the table, which was a lot of money for us, for my father and me and Jenny, anyway, even if it was nothing to Curtis Smith. When she turned her back, I snatched two dollars from the table, and the bum, leaning back in his chair and looking full and satisfied, winked at me as if we were both in the same business of taking whatever we could get.

4

We didn't talk much on the way to Oak Groves. The rain had become a fine, grainy mist that speckled the windshield, and I was thinking about the dead man. I didn't know anything about him, even though he'd had everything to do with what was happening now. He was making my father unlovable. He was making my mother decide to go with a man called Curtis Smith, whom she barely knew. A dead man was doing this. 'Who was Mr. Warner?' I asked.

'He liked to be called Colonel Warner,' she said. 'When he could recognize his name, anyway. He didn't always know you were trying to talk to him. If he did understand that he was being addressed, he wasn't very nice to you.' She paused. 'He was no one, really.'

'Who was he?' I asked.

'Does it really matter?' she asked me. 'You're making me need to smoke again.' She took out a cigarette and lit it.

'Can I say the Ten Commandments now?' Jenny asked from the backseat.

'No,' my mother said. 'Mr. Warner ... Colonel Warner was alone. That's for sure,' she said. 'He was ninety-two last Wednesday and had no one in the world save for a stepsister in Reno who did not once come to visit him and who was pretty interested when we called her this afternoon. She must have known that she'd get whatever money he had left to his name. Maybe his wife really loved him when she was still alive. He'd sometimes talk to her in the tearoom as if she were sitting across the table from him. He'd say, 'Oh, Martha, not again. Please. How many times do I have to tell you?' as if he were really disappointed in her for doing something he didn't like for the thousandth time, like putting too much sugar in his coffee or overcooking the chicken. But they might have really loved one another. He was retired military, and they paid for him to be at Oak Groves. Oak Groves is not cheap, you know. But he had no one,' she said again, her voice soft and spooked. 'Not a single soul.'

'Was he in a war?' I asked her.

'More than one,' my mother said. 'I think he was in all the big ones. He used to talk about the Adriatic Sea as if it were out in front of Oak Groves. I wonder what war happened on the Adriatic Sea,' my mother said. 'He would wake up at night from dreams. He'd be afraid, and I could tell it was because of the wars. It was a specific kind of fear. You could see that in his face. He would be remembering something terrible, something worse than most people ever have to experience, and you couldn't tell him anything that would make it better. I don't think he understood much of what anybody said to him at the end. All you could do was hold him for a while. He liked that. His wife must have done that for him.'

'Where's the Adriatic Sea?' I asked her. I was glad we weren't talking about her leaving my father anymore. I half believed that it might disappear if we didn't think or talk about it. So instead I thought about the vastness of the world, the places I might see someday, especially if I became a pilot. I thought about war – the fear and death of war – which wasn't really a terrible thought since I could hardly imagine it, since it happened in places like the Adriatic Sea, which must be very beautiful, must have that quietness and peace of any place where terrible things once happened but were now only a memory.

'Hmmm,' my mother said, looking out the windshield as if she were trying to spot somewhere in the gray drizzle what I'd imagined would be a brilliant, glassy expanse of translucent ocean blue that might, in an instant, be rippled by a sudden sea wind. 'Somewhere else,' she said. 'Somewhere far away from here. Maybe in the Middle East. It sounds biblical to me.'

'No,' Jenny said, as if she were the expert. 'That's the Dead Sea. That's the sea of the Bible.'

'There's more than one sea in the Bible,' I said, though in truth I had no idea. I had never read the Bible.

'He was very much alone,' my mother said, returning to a familiar thought. 'More than I can even imagine.'

I wanted to know more about Colonel Warner, but I didn't want to have to keep hearing about how he had no one, how alone in the world he was.

'The Ten Commandments start with Moses,' Jenny said, 'when he brought them on stone to the people wandering in the desert.'

'Mom said *no*,' I said. If you gave Jenny a chance to be in the spotlight, she would take it, and I was in no mood to give her all the attention she wanted that afternoon.

'Go ahead, Jen-Jen,' my mother said. 'What are the Ten Commandments?' I could tell she didn't really want to know. She was just trying to relieve her guilt for everything she'd done and was still going to do to us that day.

'Thank you,' Jenny said. And then, as we were barreling down Seventh East in the rain, getting closer to Oak Groves, Jenny started going through them, very slowly and carefully. 'One,' she said. 'I am the Lord thy God, which have brought thee out of the land of Egypt, and thou shalt have no other gods before me. Two: Thou shalt worship no idols or graven images, for I the Lord thy God am a jealous God. Three: Thou shalt not take the name of the Lord thy God in vain.' As she gradually worked through each phrase, each shalt and shalt not, her voice took on a strange depth. Her articulation became solid and distinct and powerful, as if some chilly, distant voice, not quite my sister's, spoke the commandments through her. There was something remedial and balanced about each sentence, and this quality seemed to have taken hold of her. It was unsettling. It made me wonder what had suddenly happened to the frivolous, happy drill team member that my sister had recently become. 'Five: Honor thy father and thy mother,' she said. 'Six: Thou shalt not covet thy neighbor's oxen or his wife.' She hesitated. 'No,' she said. 'That's not six. Six is not killing. Thou shalt not kill.'

As she continued, I realized that I didn't really know the Ten Commandments. I knew some of the basic ones: Thou shalt not kill, for example. But my knowledge went no further than that. I understood that my mother did not really know them, either, since she hardly seemed to expect what Jenny was about to say in her weird, chilly voice as soon as we had pulled into the parking lot of Oak Groves. 'Thou shalt not commit adultery,' she said three or four times, until my mother turned around and said, 'Shut up, Jenny. Please, shut up.' Jenny shut up then, though that didn't keep me from wondering what our ignorance of these laws meant about us, even if I didn't believe in God or an afterlife or any kind of divine justice – at least, I didn't think I believed in it. As we sat in our parked car looking out into the rain, I had to ask myself the very stupid question of how my family would have been different if we actually knew those ten laws and lived by them. It was pretty obvious to me that if that were the case we wouldn't have been the Parkers at all. We would have been an entirely different family. And because that thought led absolutely nowhere, I put it out of my mind.

All the same, I had to ask Jenny a question that was

itching away at me. 'What about loving your neighbor as you love yourself?' I asked. 'What number commandment is that?'

'That's not a commandment,' she said. 'That's something Jesus said later.'

'Oh,' I said.

Oak Groves didn't have any Oaks. It didn't have any trees at all, which made sense because Salt Lake is basically on the edge of a desert, and aside from the pine trees that you see in the mountains, there aren't that many trees. The name was a cover-up for what was nothing more than a number of small, square buildings called facilities. The buildings were linked by sidewalks on which two men in white were quickly pushing an empty hospital bed through the rain. Nurse Brown met us at the front desk of facility Number Six, where my mother had been bathing Mr. Warner when he fell on her and died. Nurse Brown was a large woman with short black hair and a bloodred mole about the size of a pebble on her upper lip. 'Where have you been, Mary?' she asked. 'We have people waiting for us.'

'I'm sorry, Betty,' my mother said. 'I was taking care of family matters.'

'*I'm sorry* is not what I need to hear right now.' The nurse glanced over at Jenny and me – the family matters, her eyes seemed to label us.

'This is Jenny and Steven,' my mother said awkwardly. 'My kids.' She didn't need to think at all about what she said next. She just said it. 'I'm quitting, Betty. I'll go do whatever I need to do. After that, I'm afraid I'm done.'

'We would have appreciated two weeks' notice. You realize that you're jeopardizing us.

'I wish I could do that,' my mother said. 'But not after Mr. Warner. It's not my kind of work.'

Nurse Brown sighed. 'Yes,' she said. 'I guess we all saw that.' She looked over at Jenny and me again. She had a wide chin and a single eyebrow and a large, indistinct bust that seemed too solid to be a woman's breasts. She wore the same all-white nurse's uniform that my mother did, and a small black walkie-talkie clipped to her belt. Looking at her, you got the impression that she'd seen hundreds of old people die without flinching, and that she was ashamed of my mother's squeamishness, her girlish, nonsensical fear of death. Her eyes, quick and unkind, moved from my head to my feet and back up again, and I felt myself bristle, as if touched in an unpleasant way. She did the same to Jenny. She distrusted us. She distrusted all kids, I guessed. 'Will your children behave themselves if we leave them on their own for a while?'

'Yes,' Jenny said. 'We will.'

'I am talking to your mother,' Nurse Brown said.

'They are very well behaved,' my mother said.

'What happened to him?' Nurse Brown asked. I looked down at myself as I often did when people asked about my arm.

'Just an accident,' my mother said. I wondered then why we never told the truth. Why didn't we just say that

I'd been given a thorough beating by another boy my age? I sometimes just wanted to say it outright, to tell everybody that some stupid kid had kicked the shit out of me.

'Well,' Nurse Brown said, 'you will probably be happy to know that I got some other girls to prepare Colonel Warner. He's cleaned up. We just need a report from you.' She was looking at me while she talked about Colonel Warner's body, how it had been prepared. It was terrible. I wanted her to look away, to stop bothering me with her eyes that knew so much. 'They can wait in the game room for you. Mrs. Smith and Mr. Alan are in there. They won't mind, so long as Jenny and Steven behave.'

When my mother, startled and worried, looked at me then, I knew right away that the Mrs. Smith in the game room was the mother of her lover, Curtis Smith. I didn't want to meet the old woman, especially in this strange way, and both my mother and I must have squirmed in our places. But Nurse Brown was not the sort of person to be directed by signals and undercurrents. 'This way,' she said to Jenny and me.

The hallways were windowless and brightly lit by buzzing, white fluorescent lights reflected by the white walls and white waxed floors. The floors shone with an icy veneer of brightness that seemed almost dangerous to walk over. At intervals on either side of us were closed doors behind which, I knew, old people lay sick and frail or maybe just resting, napping. An ancient person – man or woman, I could not tell – motored past us in an electric wheelchair, a blue, veiny hand pressing forward on the joysticklike knob on the chair's armrest. As the chair whizzed by, Jenny took my arm. 'This is freaky,' she whispered.

'There is nothing to be afraid of,' Nurse Brown said. She had somehow heard Jenny's whisper, despite the fact that Jenny had spoken in a barely audible voice. 'If you just mind yourselves, that is,' she added.

Nurse Brown ushered us through the door of the game room. 'Wait here,' she said. 'Your mother will come for you later.' Then she was gone.

The room was entirely white as the whole facility seemed to be. At the center of the whiteness, surrounded by two Ping Pong tables, a Foosball game, and a number of chairs, Mrs. Smith sat alone at a large round table looking into the air. Jenny was staring at her, studying her, just as I was. She must have noticed our mother's nervousness and made her own conclusions. 'Is that her?' she whispered.

'Who?' I said, wanting to pretend ignorance.

'You know.'

I sat down directly across from the old woman while Jenny wandered over to Mr. Alan, who sat behind Mrs. Smith and me at a card table playing checkers with himself. 'King me,' he said triumphantly. He turned the board around after each move and his voice changed, higher or lower, depending on whose turn it was. 'Go ahead,' he said as he carefully turned the board around once again and considered the next move he would make against himself. My sister, in her overfriendly way, sat down opposite him and said, 'Hi, Mr. Alan. I'm Jenny Parker. My mother works here. It's nice to meet you.'

Mr. Alan wore baby blue pajamas and one of those plastic hospital bracelets on his wrist. Fuzzy patches of gray hair were scattered across his thin scalp. 'Excuse me,' he said to Jenny, 'but I am sitting in that seat.' Jenny looked down at her lap, puzzled. 'Up,' he said.'Up . . . up.' Jenny stood up and hovered around his table now until Mr. Alan, still not pleased, shooed her away with a hand.

'He's strange,' Jenny said, sitting down next to me.

'He's just old,' I said, though I was in the middle of my own odd encounter. For the last thirty seconds at least, Mrs. Smith had been staring at me, though she didn't seem to see me. She saw past me with her bright, glassy eyes. She was dressed meticulously in a gray suit with a silver brooch on her jacket and a gray scarf draped over her shoulders. She might have been decked out for an occasion of some sort. Her hands were on the table, and I could see the slightest trembling in her liver-spotted fingers, though her nails were manicured and painted. I put a hand up and waved at her.

'Hi,' Jenny said.

She made no sign of seeing us, though finally she nodded and smiled at no one. 'Please pass the potatoes, if you would, dears,' she said, not seeming to speak to Jenny or me. I hardly knew what to do. There was nothing on the tabletop. 'Crown me!' Mr. Alan shouted out from the other side of the room. 'Oh, damn you!' his other, higher voice said, angered and defeated. 'Please pass the potatoes, if you would, dears,' Mrs. Smith said again with the same vacant shine in her eyes. I looked over the table again, feeling a little frightened, trapped by the emptiness I saw there. There were no potatoes. I looked back up at her: her face was ghostly pale, the silvery color of moth wings.

'She wants you to have dinner with her,' Mr. Alan said, surprising me with his sanity. 'You shouldn't sit there. She'll do that to you every time. You're just going to have to pass the potatoes now. It wouldn't be fair to disappoint her, would it?'

'I get it,' Jenny said. Then she reached out into the air in front of her, picked up the potatoes and passed them.

'Don't do that,' I said. It bothered me. There were no potatoes and we had no obligation to amuse a crazy old woman.

Mrs. Smith now looked directly at me – though still without seeming to see me – and said, 'Please pass the potatoes, dear.' I looked down at my hands. I didn't want to do it, but I did it anyway. I reached out and passed the potatoes. 'Thank you, dear,' she said.

'You're welcome,' I said, not sure why I was being polite.

After a moment, she nodded and said, 'Please pass the green beans, dears,' and Jenny and I both reached out, took the nonexistent beans, and passed them. 'So very kind of you,' she said.

'You're welcome,' I said, after which Jenny said the same thing.

Nodding again, she said, 'Please pass the mutton, if you

would, dears.' Of course, we did. She said thank you in her roundabout way and we said you're welcome, even though we had absolutely no reason to be polite to this stranger. The game continued. Whatever dinner we were having, it was large and included every food you could think of – yams, stuffing, sweet potatoes, mashed potatoes, cranberry sauce, dark gravy, blond gravy, pumpkin soup, noodle soup, beef barley soup, potato salad, Jell-O salad, three-bean salad, coleslaw, pumpkin, pecan, cherry, apple, chocolate, and banana cream pies. There was no end to the dishes, and as Jenny and I passed them and said you're welcome, Mr. Alan continued his campaign against himself at the checkerboard, carefully turning the board around and speaking to himself in two distinct voices – the voice of the winner and the voice of the loser. The odd thing was that old Mrs. Smith, tiny and withered, so thin that you could see the cords and knotty cartilage in her neck bob as she spoke, was obviously not a big eater. She never once moved her hands or pretended to help herself to the dishes. Instead, she surveyed the table where she seemed to see a number of people stuffing themselves with food as it came around. There was a twinkle of satisfaction in her eyes, a deep happiness at whatever it was she had created for herself. Meanwhile, as she asked for dish after dish to be passed, her hands lay in front of her, barely trembling. It might have been Thanksgiving or Christmas or Easter dinner or some combination of all those dinners. 'You're welcome,' Jenny and I kept saying. 'You're welcome. You're welcome.'

It wasn't until Mr. Alan stood up and began to inch out of the room with his walker that I started to feel hateful toward old, crazy Mrs. Smith. 'Damn it to hell,' Mr. Alan was saying in defeat as he slowly made his way out of the game room. I had to wonder why he'd decided to get up from that table as the loser, since he had won there, too, and could have left the room in victory. I had to wonder that, just as I had to wonder why my sister and I were being so damn cordial to this woman. She was Curtis Smith's mother, after all, and for some stupid reason I was at her family dinner. I was making her happy, and it made no sense at all. And after Mr. Alan took what seemed like five minutes to leave the room, I looked right at the old woman's face and refused her most recent request. 'No,' I whispered at her. But she just asked for the collard greens again, a food I didn't even know existed. Jenny looked at me, but she didn't say anything. We were all alone now, so I said it again, this time a little louder. 'No. I'm not passing the collard greens.' But nothing seemed to reach the old woman. Her insanity had sealed her away in a happiness so complete and vast that she could register nothing else.

'Steven,' Jenny said in a worried voice.

'Shush,' I warned.

Then I looked into the old woman's eyes. 'There are no stupid collard greens!' I shouted across the table at her.

She just nodded and said again, 'Please pass the collard greens, if you would be so kind, dears.'

Jenny passed them. 'There. I passed the greens.'

'There's no damn food. None!' I shouted. I slapped the empty table with my hands and finally the old woman looked a little frightened, though it was difficult to tell what she felt with all the wrinkles and creases and spots on her face.

'Don't shout at her, Steven,' Jenny said.

The old woman put a hand to her chest and swallowed, and that one gesture of shock might have satisfied me and I might have stopped there had I not noticed how her hair, white as cotton, was combed so nicely, pinned at the sides and held down by two barrettes in the same style as Jenny's hair, which my mother had done for her that morning. 'Look at her hair,' I said to Jenny.

'What?' Jenny asked.

'Don't you see it? How could you not see it?'

'Oh,' she said. 'Oh.' We both knew then that my mother had done crazy, old Mrs. Smith's hair, had done it carefully, lovingly, had combed through it and pinned and tied it back earlier that day, probably not long after she had done Jenny's hair for her, and probably before Colonel Warner had died and changed everything.

'Damn!' I said. Jenny grabbed at my arm, but I pushed her down in her chair and walked over to the old woman, stood behind her and began to pull the pins and barrettes out of her hair, at first carefully, and then fast and too forcefully. Her hands paddled up toward me, but I was out of her reach. 'Help,' I heard her say. When her hair hung down in strands over her shoulders and face, I grabbed a fistful of it and pulled until Mrs. Smith yelped. It didn't sound like a person. It was a terrible, weak cry, and I let go of her hair and backed away as quickly as I could.

'Stop,' Jenny said, even though I had already stopped.

'I'm sorry,' I said. The old woman pulled her hair away from her face and looked at me. She was afraid and had begun to cry. I had utterly destroyed whatever dream she'd been dreaming, her family dinner or whatever it was.

Jenny kneeled in front of her and began picking up the hairpins from the floor. 'Please don't cry, Mrs. Smith,' she said. The old woman's lips were trembling and wet with tears. 'My brother's sorry.' When I walked toward them again, the old woman started to shake and hold on to Jenny. 'Stay away,' my little sister said. 'You're scaring her.'

'I'm sorry,' I said again, this time apologizing to my sister, who was now combing through the old woman's hair with her hands.

'We're going to fix you up, she was saying softly to Mrs. Smith. 'We're going to do your hair up nicely again. Okay, Mrs. Smith?' Mrs. Smith nodded. She seemed to have understood my sister. Jenny kept combing through the old woman's hair, very gently and rhythmically, as she began pinning it down again. 'There,' she said. 'That's looking better, isn't it?'

'You don't have to do that,' I said, still angry. I just wondered why old Mrs. Smith should be so cared for, considering what was about to happen to our family.

'Do what?' Jenny asked.

'Her hair. You don't have to do that.'

Jenny stopped and looked at me in a way I had never seen my sister look at me before. She was disgusted. 'You can leave,' she said. 'You can please leave.'

'Leave?' I said.

'The room,' she said. 'Get out. Leave.' I didn't know what to do. I looked back at the open door behind me. I had always been the one to tell my little sister what to do before, to tell her how to behave. 'We don't want you here,' Jenny said.

'You're nothing,' I said to Jenny. 'You're just a stupid Billmorette. A drill team girl.' I could hardly believe how dumb I sounded.

'Bye,' she said, waving a hand at me. Her gaze was cruel and dismissive.

'I'm sorry,' I said again. And then I turned around and left.

I followed the bright hallways for a while – they seemed to go on and on – trying not to think of what I'd just done, the look of terror on old Mrs. Smith's face, the anger and disgust in my sister's. I saw a number of old people and a nurse or two, though no one wondered why I was there or asked me who I was. I must have looked like anyone's visiting grandson, so much so that one old man hugged me in the middle of the hallway. He was dressed in the same loose blue pajamas that Mr. Alan had been wearing, the uniform at Oak Groves. I stood stiffly and received his embrace. He smelled dirty, of body odor, of mustiness and old age, though his ashy hair was nicely combed and he looked clean. In the hand he wasn't hugging me with, he held a metal pole on wheels from which hung a transparent bag of some liquid – urine or IV fluid, maybe. A tube ran from it and into the loose top of his pajamas. He released me and looked at me, taking me in, beholding me as if I were too much glowing light, a miracle, his old, wide eyes full of shameless love. He called me a boy's name that wasn't mine. 'No,' I said. 'That's not me.' But he wouldn't listen. He had a soft, chubby, teddy-bear face, and he kept touching me, shaking my hand, caressing my arm, sort of petting me, as if I'd disappear if he let go. 'Your grandma's here somewhere,' he said. 'We have plans for you. We've been discussing them all week. Great plans,' he said. His eyes glowed with some ridiculous vision of the time we would spend together. 'You're a lovely boy. Lovely. Where is your grandma?' I knew she was dead. It was obvious. He was adrift without her. And as he looked around, calling out her name and seeming frightened by her absence, he gripped my arm tightly, anchoring himself. 'She's always off somewhere,' he said. 'Oh, well.' He looked at me with a terrible neediness now, and I almost wanted to stay because he believed in me. His conviction that we belonged together seemed that absolute.

I had to yank my arm out of the old man's grip and move quickly. 'Boy,' he said. He followed me but was too slow, inching along with his metal post in tow. He shouted the same boy's name – not mine – down the hallway at me, his old voice cracked with heartbreak.

I was still trying not to think of old Mrs. Smith, how I'd terrorized her, ruined her hairstyle, bullied her into crying, and turned Jenny against me. I was used to being a good kid. My father was a slob, a slob with a big heart whom I loved more than anyone. But nonetheless a slob. And so I had to be good. I had to be the one to make Jenny study and finally earn the Bs she'd promised months ago to earn. I had to be the one to make sure my father would stop spending money. I had to be the one to make sure our mother wouldn't finally make good on what she had promised to do for years now and leave him. I had to be the one to make sure she remained forward-looking and kept on loving him whether he deserved it or not. But now that she had taken a lover, now that she had groomed and cared for Curtis Smith's old, insane mother, she was no better than he was. And now that I'd done what I'd done, I was bad, too. We had all sunk into it, and I wasn't sure what was left to save now.

I wandered around until I found a storage room where dozens of collapsed gurneys and folded-up wheelchairs and metal poles on wheels for IV and urine bags were kept. I unfolded a wheelchair, sat in it, and began to push myself around in the empty center of the room. Closing my eyes, I imagined that I was a cripple, that I could do nothing else but sit and feel the soft press of gravity. My legs felt leaden and dead. Upturned in my lap, my good hand was absolutely immovable – a cold piece of flesh. For a moment, I felt the weird sensation of my neck and face,

the only vital, prickly parts of me. It was a terrible feeling.
So I went back to being a kid who was just playing around
in a wheelchair, being a troublemaker for once in his
stupid, well-behaved life, misbehaving exactly as Nurse
Brown had feared he would.

I wheeled myself over to a large stainless steel refrigerator against the wall and pulled it open. Inside in a
metal rack were dozens of glass containers – urine samples
of everyone in Facility Six – labeled and arranged in
alphabetical order. WARNER, H., COL., said the label on
old Mr. Warner's vial. I tried to review the Ten
Commandments quickly in my head and was able to
remember some of them – '*Thou shalt not commit adultery*',
for instance – though I couldn't remember if '*Thou shalt
not steal*' was one or not. It certainly seemed like one of
the ten. But, as far as I knew, it might have been something Jesus said or just a rule, a law, something that
everybody knew but that nobody in particular – God or
Jesus or anybody – had said. I wanted it to be a
commandment because when I took Mr. Warner's vial
out of the rack and zipped it up in my coat, as I did then,
I wanted it to matter. I wanted it to change something. I
wanted that little theft to be a desecration, the most
terrible violation of Oak Groves, of Colonel Warner
himself, of my mother and Curtis Smith and his mother,
of everyone, all humanity. At the time, I could think of
nothing worse to do. And that's why I stole the old man's
urine. I was going bad, getting used to it, I thought, and
this would be my pact with the devil, the act that would

change my allegiances forever, even though it was just a stupid act of vandalism, and I half knew it.

With that small item zipped into my coat, I walked through a set of double doors and down a corridor and through another set of double doors where a nurse finally stopped me. 'Who are you?' she asked.

I didn't think I could tell her. Not at that point. 'I don't know,' I said.

She laughed awkwardly, led me down another hall, and asked me to take a seat. She would be back in a minute. Without thinking, I followed her instructions. I sat down and picked up a book called *Talking to Your Elderly Parent about Money*. 'If talking about money has been something your parent just can't seem to do,' the first sentence read, 'you should keep in mind that often their silence has to do with a generation gap. Many older people were reared and brought up in an age in which money was a taboo subject.'

I closed that book, realizing that sitting there waiting to be identified was not the best idea. So I moved on, walking through one and then another set of double doors and down a number of windowless hallways and through a few windowless rooms, wondering where everybody was, wondering where the rooms with windows began, where I might find a place to look at the world outside the blankness of Oak Groves. I wanted that place to fulfill at least the smallest part of what its name promised. I wanted there to be oaks at Oak Groves. I wanted it to have rows and rows of those trees – thickly leaved, sleepy giants that turned golden in the fall and exploded in the spring. I wanted there to be miles of green lawn and hedges and flowers where old people could wander and gather in times of good weather. And when the weather was no good – as it was that day – at least they could look out at the gray winter grounds and imagine it in summer. But I couldn't find one window in that place.

I walked down one corridor after another and through one more set of double doors and into an unlit room where I just stood in the dark. Oak Groves was so white, so glaringly white. The walls and floors and ceilings were white. Everything exposed, naked, with no shadows. My eyes felt scorched, burnt out. I was tired of seeing so damn much, and I understood why my mother hated her job. I maybe even began to understand why she would do just about anything to get out of the place. And so I stood there looking into the shapeless dark, adjusting to it as things – tables, counters, a chair, and then another chair – began gently emerging from all that soft, contourless nothing. I thought then that if you ever had to fall into nothing, if you had to die and experience nothing, a nothing of darkness would be much more bearable than a nothing of light. That would be my preference, anyway. I had a moment or two more with that thought before the doors flung open and the world exploded, suddenly bright. I squinted and put a hand above my eyes the way you'd do to keep the sun away, though it had no effect in the whiteness of Oak Groves. In front of me stretched over a table lay old Colonel

Warner's body, covered in a green hospital blanket up to his naked shoulders. His forehead was huge and as white as an unused bar of soap, with the same waxy, clean texture. Thick black hair grew from his ears, which were large and wooden-looking with rubbery lobes. I knew it was Colonel Warner because he was dead and because on top of a box of clothes at the end of his table lay a dark blue military jacket, glittering with decorations. He had been a tall man and his feet stuck out of the blanket, one of them bare, bleached like a sun-dried bone, and the other covered in a black sock that stopped just below his white knee. 'What are you looking at?' Nurse Brown asked me. Her face expressed disgust. 'Did you do that?' she asked. 'Did you put that sock there?'

'No,' I said.

She walked over to the colonel, removed the sock from his foot, and put it in the box. She blamed me. I could see that in her face. She thought that I had put that sock on the dead man's foot. How she could have thought that I didn't know, except that her belief in the corruption of children went far deeper than I could ever imagine. God, how I wished she hadn't removed that sock from old Colonel Warner's foot. The socked foot hadn't bothered me so much. But the naked one had, and I'd wanted her to find the other sock and put it on him. Then I wanted her to find his other things in that box – his boxer shorts, his white button-up shirt, his necktie, his dark blue military pants, his shoes, and finally his decorated jacket – and put them on him one by one until Colonel Warner was dressed as if for dinner or formal tea or even war, for anything that a military officer did.

'Stop that staring,' Nurse Brown said.

I couldn't take my eyes off him. I just had to look at him and keep on looking at him until I was sick. My face heated up and sweat beaded my forehead. I felt that deep, painful movement in my gut. It came over me too suddenly, too powerfully to control – a pinprick of heat that blossomed and gushed out. My stomach muscles clenched as hot liquid seeped into my pants. I had shat myself. I looked down, and Nurse Brown, who saw people do that sort of thing daily, knew right away what had happened. 'Well,' she said, taking me by the hand and pulling me along, 'it looks like you've made a mess.'

'I'm sorry,' I said. I could not believe the sound of my own voice – the smallness of it. Nurse Brown marched on, gripping my hand firmly in hers until she left me at the door of a large closet. 'Don't move,' she said. She came out with a folded pair of sky blue Oak Groves pajamas and a roll of white plastic garbage bags. As we walked, I smelled myself – the simple, unmistakable smell of shit – and felt it trail down my legs and touch my socks. 'I'm sorry,' I said again, and felt as though I were apologizing for a great deal more than messing myself, though I was not about to admit to terrorizing the old woman or stealing Colonel Warner's urine.

'We're not a day care center here,' she said, still marching me down the hallway.

'I know,' I said.

She must have heard something in my voice then because she changed her tune. 'A mess,' she said, 'is just a mess.

Locked inside a large shower, I undressed and deposited my jeans, underwear, and socks in one of the white garbage bags, then handed the bag off to Nurse Brown, who stood outside the door. On the wall opposite the shower, a full-length mirror reflected me – naked, tall, and skinny with a film of gray liquid running down my legs. I hated my body at the age of fifteen. I hated the new patches of hair, the boniness of it, the awkward dangly limbs. I tried not to look, but I was no more capable of looking away from that strange sight than I had been of looking away from the colonel. As I breathed in the thick odors of shit, I thought of the singing bum and tried to hum, as he had, the melody to 'Stormy Weather' but produced only cracked, splintered tones – noise and not music. I gave up on feeling better about anything that had happened that day and went limp beneath the hot drum of water from the showerhead.

When I stepped back into the hallway, I was dressed in the blue pajama bottoms worn by every old man in that place. Luckily, my red winter coat with the vial of Mr. Warner's urine zipped into the pocket and my T-shirt that said TEAM PLAYER on it distinguished me from the two old men who were just then dawdling by. 'Here,' Nurse Brown said, handing me my dirty clothes, which she had double-bagged in the white garbage liners so that, I guessed, the stink wouldn't get out. Dressed in the uniform of Oak Groves and carrying my shitty clothes in a bag, I followed Nurse Brown.

She took me back into the front room where Jenny sat now looking down at her lap. 'I caught your sister playing with Mrs. Smith's hair,' Nurse Brown said. 'I'm afraid you two are just going to have to sit here until your mother is done. And I mean sit. I don't want you doing anything else, and I don't want you going anywhere. Understood?'

Jenny lifted her head and nodded at her. 'Understood,' my sister said.

I knew that Jenny had not ratted on me, and I was thankful. All the same, I refused to play the part of a five-year-old. 'Whatever,' I said, which was a favorite word of mine in those days.

'Sit down,' Nurse Brown commanded, pointing to the seat next to Jenny. I sat down and put the bag with my shitty clothes on the chair next to me. 'And don't go anywhere.' As she said those words, I looked right at the part of her mouth with the bloodred mole and watched the mole twitch as her mouth moved. Then her mouth was gone, and once again Jenny and I were alone.

'Thank you for not saying anything,' I said, not looking at Jenny.

'What happened to you? Where are your clothes?'

'Nothing happened to me.'

'Your hair is wet,' she said. 'You smell like soap.'

'I just washed my hands.'

Jenny poked at the garbage bag. 'Are your clothes in

there? Did you get sick or something?'

I moved the bag away from her. 'I just washed my stupid hands.'

She was too tired to keep on bugging me about something I wasn't going to tell her. 'I would have told,' she said. 'I wanted to. But I didn't know how to say it. It was too terrible to say about you.'

'I'm sorry,' I said.

'I don't understand you. I don't understand why you did that to Mrs. Smith.'

'I said I was sorry.'

'You were really trying to hurt her.' I could hear from her voice that Jenny was still shaken. 'I didn't know who you were. I didn't recognize you.'

'I wasn't thinking, I guess.' She didn't say anything for a while. 'I was still me. I wasn't anybody else or anything.'

'You were such a bully.' That comment bothered me. It made me think of Danny Olsen and what he had done to me and how my sister seemed to think I had done the same to old Mrs. Smith. 'You were worse than a bully.'

'I had to do something,' I said. 'That was that man's mother.'

'She was an old woman,' Jenny said. She actually stood up and moved a seat away from me.

Seeing her move, seeing the empty seat open up between us, I became anxious about all the wrongs I'd committed that day. 'Jenny,' I said. 'I shouldn't have done it.' She looked away from me then, and someone down the hallway, in a place where we could no longer go now that we had been grounded to the reception area, screamed loudly, almost insanely. God, did I want to leave that place. 'I just sort of lost it. I wish I hadn't acted like that. I wish I hadn't scared her. I just wasn't thinking, Jenny.'

Jenny turned a little toward me. 'Are you thinking now?' she asked.

'Sure,' I said. 'I'm thinking.'

She sat next to me again and put her head on my shoulder. 'I'm scared,' she said.

'I know.'

'Is this really happening?'

'No,' I said. 'I mean, I'm not going to let it happen. I'm going to do whatever I have to do to keep it from happening.'

'Maybe we shouldn't do anything,' Jenny said. She was tired and yawned and rubbed her nose against my shoulder. 'Maybe we should just see what happens.'

Then she lifted her watch and said the time out loud, which she'd gotten in the habit of doing as a way of showing off her new Swatch. 'It's half past five already.'

That's when I thought about our father at home. He'd been home all afternoon on what was supposed to be one of his days for studying. He was probably wondering where we were, since Mom usually arrived home by four-thirty. He was probably worried about us. He was probably looking around him at the empty house and starting to feel alone and left out and maybe irritated. 'We should call Dad,' I said.

'Nurse Brown said we couldn't leave our seats,' Jenny said. When I got up anyway and walked behind the unmanned reception desk and picked up the telephone, Jenny grabbed on firmly to her chair handles and said, 'I'm not getting up. I'm staying right here.'

'Since when have you been so determined to follow the rules?' I asked.

'Things are too crazy.'

The phone rang almost five times before he picked up. 'Yep,' he said.

'Yep,' I said back to him, a little annoyed because he was supposed to say 'Parker residence' or, at the very least, hello, which even Jenny was capable of doing.

'Yep,' he said.

'Yep,' I said.

'Is this a prank call?' He sounded annoyed.

'Hi, Dad.'

'Oh,' he said, 'it's you.'

'I thought I'd call to let you know where we were.'

'Uh-huh.' I could hear the TV in the background, and I could tell that he was more interested in whatever he was watching than in talking to me.

'How are you?'

'I'm dandy,' he said. 'I'm watching pregame stuff right now and eating a little popcorn. It's the Jazz versus the Bulls, and things are going to get started in about a half hour. You and me can watch it as soon as you get home.'

'It's *you and I*, Dad,' I said. I couldn't help myself. Sometimes I just wanted my father to speak correctly.

Sometimes I just wanted him to be studying on his stupid study days and not to be watching basketball.

'What?'

'*You and I can watch it as soon as you get home,*' I said. 'That's how you say that. Not *you and me.*'

'You're acting uptight, kiddo,' he said. 'I talk the way I talk.' He ate some popcorn. 'God, did you know that Malone is shooting nearly seventy percent right now?' I didn't say anything. His carefree tone pissed me off. He'd been sitting on his ass for hours, I knew. 'Hello. You there?'

'You flunked,' I said.

'What?'

'Mom showed me your report card. You got one D– and two Fs.'

'Where the hell's your mother, Steven?' He wasn't chewing on popcorn, and I had the feeling that he wasn't watching TV anymore. He was mad.

'She said it cost us three thousand dollars, Dad. That was our money. It belonged to all of us.'

'Hey,' he said. 'You knock that off. You knock it off right now. You put your mother on the line this minute.'

He was a lousy disciplinarian. He'd never been able to wield authority very convincingly. 'Mom can't talk right now,' I said.

'What's going on?' he asked. 'Why aren't you all home yet?'

I felt my forehead heat up and my face flush. I wasn't sure that I could tell him, even though I knew he needed to hear it. I wasn't sure I could even open my mouth.

'Steven,' he said. 'Hello.'

I swallowed. 'Somebody died,' I said.

'What?' he said.

'She can't talk to you because somebody – an old man at Oak Groves – died while she was working here today. She's doing something right now that has to do with the dead guy. She's doing paperwork or something. He fell on her and died while she was giving him a bath this morning.'

'I hope your mom's okay,' he said. 'I guess that stuff happens in those places.' He actually put some popcorn in his mouth and began eating it. 'So when will you be home?'

'She's not okay,' I said. 'Nothing is okay.'

'What's that mean?' he said through a mouthful of popcorn.

'You don't know?' I asked. I still couldn't tell him, and I hoped that Mom had left a note or a phone message or something that might have given him an idea of the situation, that might have put her notion in his head so that I didn't have to be the one to say it.

'Know what?'

'I thought Mom might have hinted at it or something earlier.'

'Hinted at it?' His voice was worried.

'Or something,' I said.

'Something? Something what? Hey, Steven. Earth to Steven. This is ground control. You out there?'

This was an old game we used to play when I was younger because I had been – and still was, really – such a space-cadet kid, always zoning out and daydreaming and reading sci-fi novels and comic books. 'Yeah,' I said. 'I'm here.'

'What's it like up there? You see the moon? You see any stars?'

'Nope,' I said. 'I just see space. It's dark.'

'Oh,' he said. He could tell I didn't want to play that game. 'So what's going on, Steven? What's happening? Where the hell are you?'

'How's Noir?' I asked, because I knew that my dog must have been lonely tied up in his little backyard. I knew he was waiting for me to come home and was probably confused about my not being there.

'Steven,' my father asked, 'what's going on?'

'I'll tell you if you tell me how Noir is.' I knew that from where he sat in front of the TV he could just turn around and see Noir through the sliding-glass door.

'I guess he's okay,' my father said. 'He's tangled up in his chain again, of course.'

I didn't like the thought of Noir out there wrapped up in his chain. 'Would you please go untangle him?'

'He doesn't care, Steven,' my father said. 'If I go out there and untangle him, he'll just walk around for a few minutes until he ties himself up again.'

'Please,' I said. 'Then I'll tell you.'

'All right,' my father said. While he was gone, I turned around and faced Jenny, who was still pretty tense and holding on to her chair handles with both hands.

'Somebody's going to catch you,' she said.

'I've got to tell him.'

'What if they catch you?'

'Let them catch me.'

'There,' my father said. 'He's untangled.'

'Thank you.' I meant it. I was glad that Noir wasn't trapped and hunkered down in that stupid chain anymore.

'So what the hell is happening?'

'Okay,' I said, 'I'm going to tell you.'

'You're making this sound bad.'

'It is sort of bad,' I said. 'Mom really got upset when Colonel Warner died on her.'

'Please tell me, for Christ's sake.' So I did. I told him how Colonel Warner fell dead on her while she was washing him and that now Mom was leaving us. He paused and took in a few breaths and said, 'She's always leaving us. You know that.'

'I think this might be different.'

He took in another deep breath and let it out slowly. I heard the TV click off. 'She doesn't have anywhere to go,' he said. 'She doesn't know anyone in this city.' I didn't know what to say. 'Say something,' he said.

'She might have found someone to know.'

'Who?' he asked.

'I'm not sure, though. Maybe she hasn't found anyone. I don't know.'

'Who?' he asked again.

'Another man,' I said. 'Maybe.'

'Oh,' he said. 'Oh.' For a long time we didn't say anything, and I just stood there in these blue hospital pajamas with my red winter coat on looking at Jenny, who was holding on to her chair with all her life, as if she were sitting over a cliff or something, as she very slowly moved her head back and forth the way you do when you tell somebody *no*. *No, no, no*, her head kept saying.

'I'm sorry,' I said.

'Don't say that. There is nothing to be sorry about. Nothing is going to happen, all right? We are going to take care of everything. Okay?' When I didn't say anything, he said again, 'Okay?'

'Okay,' I said. 'What are we going to do?'

He was quiet. 'Jesus,' he finally said. 'Jesus shit Jesus. Who? What guy?'

'I don't know yet.' I lied. 'Just a guy. He lives somewhere in the Avenues.' He made some sort of noise, and I imagined him pulling on his hair, digging into it with his hands. 'Maybe you should come over here and talk to her. We're at Oak Groves. Maybe you can change her mind.'

'I don't have the car,' he said.

'You could take a cab.'

'Jesus,' he said. 'I don't have any cash on me.'

I wasn't used to my father acting like this – so helpless – and it made me impatient. 'You can take a cab anyway.'

'All right,' he said. 'I'll do that.'

'You'd better hurry. We won't be here much longer.' Then I said, maybe because I wanted to warn him, 'She's different. She's not herself, really.'

'I'll hurry,' he said. And we hung up.

When I sat back down, Jenny wanted to talk about God again. 'Janet Spencer says,' she said, looking at me with groggy eyes, 'that if you don't live by the Ten Commandments, you won't inherit the Glory.'

She just said that out of nowhere, and I had to admit it sounded nice – inheriting the Glory – even if I had no idea what the Glory was and even if I didn't appreciate the sort of brainwashing my little sister was being subjected to. 'That's pure BS,' I said. 'Anyway, what is the Glory, and who really wants to inherit it?'

'I don't know yet,' Jenny said. 'It's just something you get from God after you die.'

I didn't know why it sounded so good to me – the Glory – but it did. Maybe because I had spent what seemed like hours – I think it had only been one hour at the most – in a place that had taught me that there was no Glory, that, at the most, there was just an endless darkness or an unbearable light and no soft, in-between spaces and no spaces above or beyond those two things. I was tired and maybe wanted to believe something, if only for a few minutes. Outside a soft drizzle still came down and a swollen sliver of red winter sun bled over the mountains and colored the air this strange, hurt, twilight color that didn't seem to belong to any hour of the day. I was cold. I felt weak and exposed in those stupid pajamas. When I looked down at the white doubled-up garbage bag, I wondered if I couldn't smell the stink of myself sealed

away in there, if some of that stink wasn't leaking out.
Then I smelled it faintly, though I think it was the thought
of that stink and nothing else that I was smelling. And
that's when I had this vision, though it was more of a
feeling than something I saw, of what the Glory was. The
Glory was hardly an eternity. It was the opposite of
eternity. It was a single moment in which I noticed all the
red evening light in the room and felt Jenny leaning
against me, felt her every breath, and heard a few mindless
bird chirps – a black string of Glory sound – coming from
some place outside – a treetop, a rain gutter – that I would
never see. It wasn't that you were going to die and go on
living for an eternity after death. It wasn't that at all. The
Glory was the way Jenny held on to my arm with her
hand. It was the way I felt the softness of her touch
through the fabric of my coat. It was the way our shadows
stretched across the room in that red light. It was the way
it no longer mattered, if only for an instant, that you
would live or die. Even though you knew something
terrible was about to happen, you didn't give a damn
about it, didn't give it a single thought, if only for a second
or two. That was the Glory and, for that instant, I knew
it. Then everything came back to me, and it was gone. I
remembered that nothing about that day was right, that
my father needed to arrive very soon, and that he probably
wouldn't make it on time, that you could count on him,
among other things, for not making it on time. Jesus,
could you count on him for that. 'There is no Glory,' I
told Jenny because I thought she had better get used to

that fact. 'There is no after you die. When you die, you die forever. You're just gone.'

'That's not what I know in my heart,' she said, nudging her forehead into my arm and seeming to position herself more deeply, more securely into the comforting world that she believed in. 'Besides,' she said, 'a lot of people believe in God.'

'A lot of people do a lot of things. Stupid things,' I added.

She sat up and looked at me. 'It's not stupid. The Spencers are nice people. A lot of Mormons are nice people.'

'This is not about the Spencers,' I said. 'This is about believing in a lie, in an illusion.'

'You're just acting like Dad,' she said. I couldn't argue with her. I did sound like our father. 'The Spencers are nice. Janet's parents never yell at each other. They really don't.'

'What does that have to do with anything? That's not even what we're talking about,' I said.

'I don't know,' she said. 'I don't know what it has to do with. It's just that they're not always arguing.'

'Jesus,' I said. 'They just believe in whatever will make them feel better. That's all they do, Jenny. That's not nice. That's just stupid.'

'You don't have to act like that,' she said. She'd heard the meanness in my voice, and she was angry with me again. 'Janet Spencer would never have done what you did to Mrs. Smith.'

'Stop talking about the Spencers,' I said. 'That's not even what we're talking about.' Her face went chilly with the look she gave me whenever she was about to subject me to the silent treatment. I hated the silent treatment. I'd rather have been hit or yelled at than been entirely ignored with the precise chilliness that Jenny had perfected. 'I don't mean to yell,' I said. 'I just wish you wouldn't believe in everything everybody tells you.' She was doing something with her hands, twiddling her thumbs. 'Jenny,' I said. She looked up at the ceiling, crossed her knees, and kicked one leg lightly as if she were having a relaxing time sitting alone somewhere. 'Don't act like a baby,' I said. She turned away from me and gazed out the window while I just sat with her and felt invisible. I waited, hoping that she would relent. But she didn't. 'I bet the Spencers yell at each other,' I said. 'I bet they do it when nobody's looking. I bet they argue a lot.' She didn't even turn her head. She just kept kicking her one leg lightly and gazing out the window at nothing.

A few minutes later, our mother came out into the reception area followed by Nurse Brown, who handed her an envelope and said, 'All right, then,' to which our mother said the same thing.

She turned around and looked at me. I stood up, holding the white garbage bag in my good hand. She had changed out of her nursing clothes, though she had forgotten to take off her little white hat. That was still there as a reminder of what she had been, and I thought it was funny that Nurse Brown hadn't said anything. I wondered if that was her way of laughing at my mother, and I didn't mind if it was. 'What happened to him?' she asked.

'An accident,' Nurse Brown said.

My mother sighed. She didn't know what sort of accident Nurse Brown meant, and she didn't seem to want to find out. She just wanted out of that place. 'He's always getting into accidents,' my mother said.

When she went for the door, I said, 'We can't go yet.'

'What's the matter with your brother, Jenny?' my mother asked.

'I don't know,' Jenny said. Then they walked through the door, and because I was not about to be left behind in that place, I followed them, thinking of my father, who always came too late.

5

'You forgot to take the hat off,' Jenny said in the car.

'Jesus,' she said, pulling it off and throwing it into the backseat as if it were diseased. 'I can't believe I did that. I can't believe I ever worked that job.'

You wouldn't have known she'd ever been a nurse by the way she was dressed now. She wore a crisp, knee-length khaki skirt that hugged her hips and emphasized the tight thinness of her middle. I'd never seen the pink blouse she wore, bright and new looking. It made me think again of how men could desire her, how they could want my mother not because her blouse was tight or suggestive, but because it was elegantly thin – you could make out the straps and lattice of her bra through the fabric – and because the brief handles of her clavicles showed in the slightly open V of her collar. She'd never looked this good around the house, and she'd never worn this particular outfit there, either. 'You look beautiful,'

Jenny said with too much enthusiasm.

'Yes,' I said in what I hoped was an accusatory tone, 'you do.'

'Thank you, Steven,' she said.

When we pulled out of Oak Groves and on to Seventh East, I looked everywhere for a sign of my father in a cab, but saw nothing. 'What's wrong with you, Steven?' my mother asked.

'I don't know,' I said.

'Sit still,' she said. She was looking into a little round makeup mirror and applying her lipstick as she drove. We were headed toward the Avenues, and something peculiar was happening with the weather. It was still drizzling, but the sun seemed to be rising and not setting. It had to do, I knew, with the descending edges of the mountains to the west so that as the sun dipped below them it seemed to ascend. It was an illusion. Still, I hadn't expected to see this giant red sun light up half the sky so that bright curtains of rain seemed to hover in the air. It was like a spring shower, only it was still February. I rolled down the window and breathed in the green, damp smell of a season that had not yet come, and wondered where the hell winter had gone. We were supposed to be hunkered down beneath blankets at home, waiting it out together, staying warm, shoveling snow, eating soup, building log fires – though we didn't have a fireplace, of course – doing whatever we needed to do to defend one another from the cold out there. It wasn't right.

I looked over at my mother and saw a magnified slice

of her mouth in the makeup mirror. She snapped it shut. 'I'm sorry if Nurse Brown was hard on you two. She is a very unhappy woman. Some people are just unhappy, and they don't know how to be anything else.' The way she said that, I understood that my mother was determined not to be one of them. That's what all this was about.

'I didn't mind Nurse Brown,' I said.

'Good,' she said. 'I'm glad my kids know how to get along. Getting along is important.' She looked over at me and glanced back at Jenny and said, 'I guess you've figured out that we're going to see Curtis now?'

'No,' I said. 'You guessed wrong.'

'Well, we are,' she said in a that's-the-way-it's-going-to-be tone of voice.

'You did that old woman's hair,' I said.

'Excuse me.'

'Didn't she, Jenny?'

Jenny was in the backseat staring out a peephole she'd made in the fogged-up window. 'I don't know,' she said.

'You do too know.'

'I don't know anything. Don't ask me anything.'

'You pulled it back and did it just like you do Jenny's hair.' I couldn't suppress a tone of viciousness. 'That crazy old woman.'

'She's senile, Steven. Anyway, it used to be a part of my job to take care of Evelyn.'

'Evelyn,' I said.

'Steven hurt her,' Jenny said then. 'Steven made her cry.'

I looked back at Jenny, amazed by what she had just said. I didn't understand. 'Whose side are you on?'

'I'm not on any side,' she said. 'You're different. You're not who you usually are.'

'Whose stupid side are you on?'

'What?' my mother asked. 'What are you saying?'

I no longer cared. I really didn't. 'I hurt her. I pulled her pretty hair out. I pulled it until she cried.'

My mother did something then that she hadn't done in years. She pulled the car over, lifted her hand, and was about to slap me when I reached up and grabbed her wrist and held it in my good hand. Even with one arm in a sling, I was stronger than she was, physically stronger, and I saw this fact for the first time and it was something I'd rather not have seen. I'd been her little boy for so long, I'd been the one who needed to be protected and kept. But in that instant, I had become something else.

'Let go of me,' she said. I heard the fear in her voice, and out of something more than shame, out of fear, too, I let go.

She drove for a while without speaking. We were cruising through the neighborhoods around Liberty Park on a weekday in the early evening, and the houses were quiet and closed up for the most part. A few people stood out on their porches looking at the rainy sky divided between light and dark, the fleshy pink underbellies of storm clouds on one side and the setting sun on the other. She finally looked at me, a slab of brightness on her face, and said, 'You need more punishment than I can give you.' She actually said that, and I knew how she felt since I also believed that she needed to be punished, severely punished, but I didn't know how to do it. Physical strength couldn't do it. I just didn't know how to hurt her as much as she was hurting me.

'I want to know everything that happened back there,' she said. 'I want to know why you are dressed in those pajamas. I want to know what you have in that garbage bag. Well,' she said, 'go ahead.'

I sat stiffly looking out the window. 'No.'

'I think I know,' Jenny said.

'You don't know,' I said.

'I think he messed his pants,' Jenny said.

'No,' I said, though I had sunk down in my seat and was cradling my hurt arm in my good one so that my whole body was an admission of guilt.

My mother was perplexed. 'What?'

'No,' I said, 'No, no, no.'

'His dirty clothes are probably in that bag,' Jenny said.

I grabbed the bag and put it on my lap and held on to it. I felt like a two-year-old. I felt like I had no secrets from anyone. 'Leave me alone,' I said. 'I got lost in Oak Groves. It's a terrible place. It really is.'

'Yes,' my mother said. Her voice was soft. 'It is. I know.'

'I got lost and went into the room where Mr. Warner . . . Colonel Warner was on a table and Nurse Brown found me there. She thought I had been putting clothes on Colonel Warner's body. She thought I'd been playing around with him. She really thought that. But I hadn't done anything. I never could have touched him. He scared me. Then I had to clean myself up.'

'Okay,' my mother said. She put her hand on the back my of head and ran her fingers softly through my hair.

'I'm sorry,' I said.

'You don't need to be sorry.'

I looked around me at the Buick, the old spacious car that my father had bought from a redheaded old lady who had been a schoolteacher and who had fed us vegetables from her garden when we came over to pick it up for a much better price than we should have gotten. A terrible thought came to me. 'Are you going to take the Buick?' I asked. That question made me feel unbearably sad.

She looked around at the car. 'I suppose the least I could do is let your father have it. He found it. It was a good find.'

'See,' I said, 'he can do things.'

I knew that she was sad, too, because she started crying the way women often cry, subtly, without any mess. I thought maybe this was my chance to change what was seeming more and more inevitable. So I said, 'What else are you going to take?'

'I wish you two would stop crying,' Jenny said, even though it was just my mother who was crying. She wasn't looking at us, and she certainly wasn't crying. She was just staring out her window.

'I'm sorry,' my mother said. 'Maybe I'm doing all of this too fast. You just have to make decisions sometimes. You just have to.' She was wiping her eyes. 'Anyway, it's you two we need to think about, not me. I've already made my decision.' I didn't know what the hell she was talking about. 'You're going to like Curtis's house. We're pretty sure all you kids will get along. It's your choice, of course. But you should realize that if you stay with your father, you'll just end up taking care of him. I know him, and so do you. That's what happened to me, didn't it? I had to take care of him, and it took every last drop of life out of me. Then you had to take care of me, and you had to take care of Jenny, too.'

'I didn't have to take care of Jenny.'

'He didn't have to take care of me,' Jenny said.

'You had to make sure she did her homework. You had to make sure she came home from school every day by a certain time. You had to tutor her in reading. You shouldn't have had to do that. One of us should have done that. You should've been off being a kid.'

'I was,' I said. 'I was off being a kid.'

'No,' my mother said. 'You weren't. You aren't. You're not happy. None of us is happy.'

'I'm happy,' Jenny said loudly.

'Shut up!' I shouted.

'This is not happy,' my mother said, shaking her head and looking hard at the road. 'I deserve to be happy. My kids deserve to be happy.'

'Fuck happy,' I said. 'Who cares about happy?'

'Steven,' my mother warned. Then she said, 'I'm sorry that you've had to take on so much more than you should have to.'

rose out of the steep slopes like small fortresses of glass. The huge windows of these houses, my father had often explained to Jenny and me, enhanced the owner's enjoyment of the city view below. He called it a million-dollar view and claimed that this view would be one among many amenities of the luxury home my family would soon own. I'd sometimes imagine us – Jenny, me, my father and mother – all sitting together, as almost never happened then, in our future living room, a ghostly space, which I could picture only vaguely, furnished with cream-colored sofas and armchairs. The carpet was also white, as were the drapes, everything white, not as that nightmare Oak Groves had been white, but a softer shade, not blank, not blinding, but a gentle, glowing, barely real white. It would be just before dark, and we'd be sitting in front of an epically large window with the city at our feet beginning to shatter into separate points of light, and just beyond it the long pink-purple smear of sunset melting to a velvet sheet of evening. Very pretty, a perfect picture, except that I hardly knew what we'd be doing with ourselves. Maybe we'd be eating black olives out of porcelain bowls and crackers smeared with whatever – salmon paste, fish eggs, goose liver – all that stuff we'd tried and hated, thrown away a few weeks before when we'd had the money to buy it on account of my arm. Only in this soft, white living room, we'd love it, we'd eat it up, and might have licked our fingers had we not known better and wiped them with cloth napkins instead. Maybe my father and mother would be playing a game of chess with marble chess pieces and a marble board, drinking red wine from wineglasses, carefully eyeing the board and being considerate, delicate, losing or winning with grace in a way that Mr. Alan at Oak Groves had not even been able to do with just himself. From time to time they would look at each other with some quiet, unspoken message, or out the window at the glittering dark of the city below or over at Jenny and me, who would also be nice as could be to each other as we played backgammon, even though we'd never played that game, just as my parents had never played chess, and didn't know the rules. There it was, all the same: we were all happy in our white room with evening coming on. For some reason, Noir wasn't there. I just couldn't place him in that picture. He hated to have to behave himself. He hated to be shut into a room where he couldn't chew on and rip apart anything he wanted to. So maybe he was out in his backyard, unchained, licking himself or killing a rodent or looking up at the birds and fantasizing about somehow reaching them, hunting them down in their sky, or maybe he was just sleeping, his head between his paws, sleeping and dreaming a dream that was probably a hell of a lot nicer than mine. Noir was secretive and without ambitions, the way animals are, so no doubt his dreams were different in ways that I could not begin to imagine. I guess even then I suspected that mine had been empty and that even my dog with his simple and very real appetites could have outdreamed me. Or maybe I didn't know that yet, maybe I had not even begun to guess it.

'I'm happy,' Jenny said quietly from the backseat, though her voice hardly sounded happy. It was small and tired and weak, and I half wanted her to intone the Commandments just to hear that strength in her voice again. 'I don't care what you say, I'm happy. I've always been happy.' Then she turned around and put her forehead against her fogged-up, rain-speckled window. No one said anything for a while. We just drove through that strange, bright evening rainstorm. I must have been pretty tired, because my eyes wanted to shut, and I had to strain to keep them open. The soft roar of the heater blowing warm air made me want to curl into myself and sleep. But I knew I had better not do that, even though I did doze off a little for about fifteen seconds or so. I remember the thought of that bum's beautiful voice humming 'Stormy Weather' and a tree or two rushing by in a golden-blue, silver-streaked sky that was not the one outside our car window but the one I had seen in Jenny's beautiful farmyard picture and that had somehow gotten into my soft, groggy mind. 'Hey,' Jenny shouted. I woke then and looked out at a different sky – still red from evening and drizzling. 'That's him. That's Dad.' She was pointing out the back window at a yellow taxicab with a man – it was our father – sticking his head out the back window, his long hair ragged and blowing in the wind. He waved a fist and shouted something I couldn't hear. Then I did hear it. 'Stop! Stop! Stop!' I don't know how he had found us, except that our old seaweed green Buick was pretty easy to pick out anywhere.

'Jesus,' my mother said. She didn't slow down. She just

kept driving as if he weren't behind us. 'How does he know where we are?'

'I called him,' I said. 'Somebody had to call him.'

'Oh,' she said. She sat back in her seat and released the gas and came to a gradual stop at the curb. 'I guess there's no point in not doing this now. We might as well get it over with.'

'What?' I asked. 'Do what now?'

'I'm sorry that you were the one to tell him, Steven. You shouldn't have had to do that. I should have done that.' There was something chilly in her voice, something I didn't like the sound of at all. 'You two might want to stay in the car.'

The cab had pulled up behind us, and my father stepped out. He was dressed in jeans and a Utah Jazz T-shirt, and his hair was soaked for some reason so that he looked half-drowned, as if he had survived a shipwreck, had just crawled out of the waves. 'We need to talk, Mary,' he said, standing in front of her door. She stepped out, and so did I. Jenny stayed in the backseat with her hands over her ears and her eyes closed. You could no longer see the light drizzle in the air, but it was coming down as we stood there. A drop or two of water fell from my father's soaked hair. One of his tennis shoes was untied, and the fat black lace was waterlogged and made me think of the bum we had seen earlier that day – the one with the plastic bags on his feet who'd worked us for three dollars with his girl-friend. I wish my father hadn't made me think of those bums, but he had.

'Hi, Billy,' my mother said. She looked over at me. 'Wouldn't you rather stay in the car, Steven?'

'I don't think so,' I said.

'I'd rather you get back in the car.'

'He can stay if he wants to stay,' my father said.

'Get back in the car, Steven.'

I didn't move. 'I'm his father,' he said. 'I say that he can stay if he wants to stay.'

'I guess you are that,' my mother said, looking at him. 'You've been a very good father, too, haven't you?' I wanted him to say something back. But he didn't. He was shivering and hugged himself with both arms and looked at her and couldn't seem to meet her gaze for very long. I didn't know where she had found a cigarette, but she had, and she lit it now in the rain, very calmly going through all the steps – putting it in her mouth, lighting the match, and bringing the weak flame to her cigarette, inhaling until it had lit, then putting the matches in her bag, snapping the clasp, and finally looking up at him as she smoked. He couldn't seem to speak until she was done with this, and I saw how already she was more powerful than he was because of the time and silence she had demanded for herself and had gotten.

'He's a good father,' I said finally.

He looked over at me. 'How's your arm, Steven?' he asked. I heard something in his voice that I didn't like the sound of – vulnerability or fear or something. 'What did the doctor say?'

'Where's your coat? You should be wearing a coat.' I

shouldn't have said that because he looked down at himself then and squeezed his arms tightly and seemed colder now. 'Your shoe is untied.' That was another thing I shouldn't have mentioned. But I wanted him to tie it so that I wouldn't have to look at him and remember the guy with the plastic sacks and his girlfriend and how they had just walked out of that restaurant with our few dollars and into the rainstorm the way someone else might walk into their living room, just walked right out into it and kept on walking. My father bent down and actually began tying his shoe. And while he was bent down working on it, the driver stood out of the cab and said, 'I have a theory about him. You want to know what my theory is?' He was skinny and wore a KISS T-shirt beneath a leather jacket, the worn shoulders of which his long, straggly black hair touched. I could tell he was a terrific asshole. My mother didn't say anything and neither did my father, who had stood up again. 'My theory is that he doesn't have any money to pay me with.'

'The doctor says that my arm is going to take a little longer to heal,' I said.

'But it's healing?' my father asked.

'Yes. I guess it is.'

'That's my theory, miss, in case you're interested.'

My mother opened her purse, took out a fifty-dollar bill, and offered it to my father. 'Hell, no,' he said. 'Hell, no. No way.' We could guess where the money had come from since my parents never carried that much cash, and I was glad he'd refused it.

'Can you pay him, Billy?' she asked.

'I think you should take it,' the driver said. He had lit a cigarette for himself. 'Otherwise, I'm just going to have to drive off and find someone else.'

My mother took a step forward and urged the bill into his hand, and my father took it and shoved it into his pocket. 'Whatever,' he said. 'Why are you dressed like that?' he asked, looking at me.

I looked down at myself and realized how terrible and out of place I must have looked in those pajamas. 'It's not important,' I said.

'Aren't you cold?' he asked, even though he was the one shivering.

'I'm fine,' I said.

He shook some water out of his head and tried to stop his upper body from trembling, though he couldn't. 'Jesus. I don't have a good feeling about this. Some guy at that home dies and you decide to leave me.'

'It's a little more complicated than that, Billy,' she said.

'What does your mother mean?' He was looking at me and not at her. 'Complicated how?' The cab driver wasn't going to sit back down in his cab and leave us to ourselves. He was smoking his cigarette and listening to the whole thing. He wasn't smiling or anything. But I knew that he was getting a kick out of it. I knew he was going to stay for the show.

'Let's keep the kids out of this, Billy.'

'Keep them out of it. I don't think that's going to be possible,' he said. 'I think they're about as much in this as they can be. Look at Jen-Jen, for Christ's sake.' He pointed to her in the backseat with her hands over her ears. She was looking out at us now and must not have heard what was being said. She sort of waved at my father with her index finger because she needed the other ones to keep herself from hearing anything.

'Steven,' my mother said, 'you get in that car now.'

'She means,' I said, 'that you need to do something with yourself and then maybe she'll come back to you.'

'That's not what I mean, Steven.'

'People die all the time,' my father said.

'It's not about that,' my mother said. 'I can't live with you anymore, Billy. That's what it's about.'

'You need to start studying,' I said to him. I had begun shivering myself now, even though I wasn't cold. 'You need to pass your classes and get your degree. You need to stop spending money all the time. You need – '

'You,' my father said in an angry whisper. 'You need to shut up.' He pointed a finger at me and stepped forward and I stepped back. He had never spoken to me like that before.

'I –'

'Not another goddamn word, kid.'

'Billy,' my mother said.

I don't know what I did next. I guess I just stood there looking into the air and feeling my mouth seize up for good, feeling the impossibility of ever again speaking to that sloppy bastard who could barely keep his shoes tied. His eyes were still locked onto me, though I wasn't meeting his gaze. I was looking at the space to the side of his head. 'You got me?' he said. I nodded, and he looked back over at my mother.

'People die every day, for Christ's sake,' my father said. 'You can quit at Oak Groves. You can work another job where people don't die.'

'You're not listening to me,' my mother said.

'You can work a job where no one has to ever die. Ever!' He was in his I-can't-shut-up mode, speaking out of panic and anger. He turned around and slapped his hands down against the cab roof and gave the car a push that made it wobble a little. He looked over his shoulder at my mother. 'Jesus. What about an office job? People don't die there? They don't die and they don't get sick behind typewriters. They don't have heart attacks or strokes or seizures. They don't need to be fed. They just sit at desks and write letters. They don't die at desks, do they? Do they?' He wanted an answer, but she wasn't going to give him one. 'They don't die in post offices or supermarkets or retail stores or restaurants or libraries or bars or cafés.'

When he finally shut up, my mother looked over at me and said, 'Please, Steven. Please let me talk to your father alone.'

'He's not leaving, Mary. He wants to stay here. He wants to know what's happening here just as much as I do. He has a right to know. We all do.'

'All right,' she said. 'You win.' She looked down at her purse and then at my father. 'I don't love you, Billy,' she said.

'That's a lie,' my father said. But he wasn't yelling now or even looking at her. He was speaking softly in the opposite direction as he leaned over the cab. He wasn't able to turn around and face us for what seemed like a long time. A few cars drove by, and one kid on a bicycle cranked up the hill and turned the corner. Otherwise, the simple houses with porches and gray windows reflecting the yellow grass of their own front yards sat quietly facing the road. No one came out of them. No one walked by. It continued to rain, and in that silence I could hear the tiny sounds of it falling.

The cab driver had gotten bored and was looking off at something else. He put his cigarette out and said, 'The meter is running, just to let you know.'

When my father finally turned around, he couldn't look at either one of us. 'Who's the man?' he asked. My mother told him more or less what she had told us in the restaurant in an equally calm voice.

'He's rich,' my father said.

'He's financially secure,' she said.

My father shook his head and started to laugh until his laugh turned into a cough and he had to stop, though he was still shaking his head. He looked down at the ground and kicked at it with his wet tennis shoe. He was smiling this very painful smile. 'Financially secure,' he said. Then he looked up at the bright, drizzling sky and shouted it. 'Financially secure! Jesus!'

'Yes, Billy,' my mother said very calmly.

The cab driver sat back down in his car and turned on

the radio or a tape that played that very sad song by Led Zeppelin – 'Stairway to Heaven'. He was moving his head to the music and very precisely lip-synching every word. I wanted to kill him.

My father was looking at me now. 'What do you think about what your mother is doing? Has she asked you what you think, Steven?'

'I thought I was supposed to shut up,' I said. He hardly knew what I was talking about. He seemed unable to remember ever having yelled at me.

'Don't you put him in the middle of this,' my mother said. 'Don't you dare do that, Billy. This isn't about the kids.'

'What do you think, Steven?' he asked.

'You don't have to answer his question,' my mother said. 'You don't have to say another word to him.'

I looked at my mother, who stood with her arms crossed, her upper body seeming to shake with anger. Then I looked back at him. 'I don't know what I think yet.' I should have said something more decisive. I should have defended my father. I should have said that what she was doing was wrong and hurtful and inexcusable.

'We've got to go now,' my mother said.

'I'll be right behind you,' my father said. 'Don't think I'm just going to let you drive away.'

'It would be better for all of us,' she said, 'if we didn't draw this out.'

'I'll be right behind you,' my father said.

I was looking at the cab driver now, whose head was

cocked back, his eyes closed as he mouthed the words
'*buying a stairway to heaven*', deep inside the ecstasy of that
song. I couldn't move or speak or think, and as disgusting
as that cab driver was with his leather coat and his KISS
T-shirt, I would not have minded being him, being where
he was in the words of that song. My mother took my
hand in hers. 'We're going now, Billy.' She walked me
over to my side and locked me in. I thought I should try
to resist her. I was fifteen, after all, and was not used to
being walked by the hand. All the same, I let her lead me
to the door and sit me down in the seat. 'Don't you follow
us, Billy.'

My father was knocking on my window. 'Steven,' he
was saying. 'Look at me. Look at me, please.' I looked at
him, but I didn't know what else to do.

'Don't either one of you dare step out of this car,' our
mother said as she started the Buick up.

'Jen-Jen,' my father said. He was knocking on both our
windows now.

'Hi,' she said, but she didn't move to open the door,
and neither did I.

He was running alongside us now as we pulled out and
I watched him looking in at us, his eyes locked on to ours
the way men and women in old movies run after a train
carrying a lover away from them. Only this was just our
father, and what I saw in his face then as he looked in at
me was not love or even desire, but fear and something
else that he was seeing about himself and that I could not
give a word to. 'I'll be right behind you,' he shouted,

pointing back at the cab. 'I'll see you in a minute.' This was not a threat. He was reassuring us. He wanted us to know that he would be nearby.

'I'll see you soon,' I shouted through the glass. And then we pulled away.

My mother was driving too fast. 'Maybe he won't follow us,' she said.

'He's going to follow us,' I said.

'You're not helping things, Steven,' she said.

'Am I supposed to help things?'

'I don't know what you're supposed to do.' Jenny and I kept turning around to look at the road. We couldn't see his cab yet, and for a frightening moment I wondered if he hadn't already given up and gone home. 'Stop that,' my mother said. 'I want both of you to sit forward and stay still.'

The next time we turned around, we saw the yellow car about two blocks behind us. It was very small and disappeared at intervals as the road rose and fell behind us. My mother looked in her mirror and saw it, too. 'Okay,' she said, not speaking to us but to him, as if he could somehow hear her. 'Fine. Fine.'

'Shouldn't we maybe stop and wait for him?' Jenny asked.

'We're not stopping,' my mother said. I saw her hands tighten around the steering wheel. 'This time, we are not stopping.' Her eyes kept lifting to the rearview mirror and then falling back down to the road in front of her.

'What are we going to do?' Jenny asked.

'We are going to get on with our lives,' my mother said. 'That's what we're going to do.' That was a funny thing for her to say since we had just then driven around the same block for the second time and were about to drive around it a third time.

'You're driving in circles,' I said.

'Yes,' she said, trying to stay calm.

'Why?' I asked.

'I'm not going to make this easy for him,' she said. 'I'm not.' He was right behind us now, so close that we could see the cab driver's skinny face appear and disappear as light fell over the windshield. My father rolled down his window and stuck his face out into the air, though he didn't say anything. I wanted him to shout or do something. But he didn't. So I rolled my window down and stuck my head out and looked at him. We were still rounding the same block, driving slowly, and the wind shook his wet hair out and made his face look paler and thinner than it was. He looked as if he had already lost us. I didn't want him to believe that. I wanted him to fight. I wanted him to do whatever was necessary. I wanted him to take action and make things right, as he had done when Danny Olsen had hurt me.

'Hi, Steven?' he finally shouted.

'Hi!' I shouted back.

'I'm sorry I yelled at you back there. I'm sorry for that.'

I didn't want him to apologize. I didn't want him to sound weak and conciliatory. I was pretty sure that he wouldn't be able to take us back if he did that. 'It doesn't matter!' I shouted.

Other than that, he didn't know what to say, and neither did I. We just looked at each other as my mother continued to drive around the same block of quiet, medium-size houses with two-car garages and dead yellow front yards and no sign of people anywhere. I wouldn't have lived in one of those houses for anything, despite the fact that they were twice or even three times the size of our duplex. 'Get back in here, Steven,' my mother said.

'Tell her I need to talk to her! Tell her that!' he shouted.

I fell back into my seat. 'He needs to talk to you.'

'I heard him,' she said. When I tried to stick my head out again, she grabbed me and held me in the car. 'We're not going to play his game,' she said.

'I'm not going to go away!' he shouted. 'I'm not. Never! Do you hear me, Mary? Do you?' His voice was broken and hoarse.

'He's going to fight,' I said. 'He is.'

My mother glanced over at me. 'So am I,' she said.

Jenny was looking out the back window at him. She waved and he waved back. 'I love you, Jenny!' he shouted, the word *love* and my sister's name half disappearing in his tired voice.

'Stop that,' my mother said. 'Stop waving at him.'

Jenny put her head down in the backseat. 'I'm closing my eyes,' she said.

looked down on the city with their black glass facades. The roads up there were both numbered and named, unlike the lower Avenues, where you just got numbers and letters. Rich people like names, of course, and no doubt they got to choose what they called their streets. The road we drove on then was called Milky Way Boulevard, and the smaller roads off Milky Way Boulevard were all named after planets – Venus, Neptune, Jupiter, and so on – which was tacky as hell, though I wasn't thinking that then. Instead, the planet names made me think about flying, about being a pilot, which was not something I thought much about anymore because I was fifteen and had poor vision and knew that I wasn't going to be a pilot. All the same, I thought back to the time, years before while we were living in Tucson, when my father took me to what was called the Bone Yard, a vast resting ground for old U.S. Air Force jets and planes no longer airworthy. The planes had been dismantled and scavenged for parts or, as our air force guide kept saying, 'cannibalized' for anything that could still be used. It was a sad and scary place – miles and miles of these aircraft, stripped of their fuselages, cockpits, wings, and wing flaps so that only their metal skeletons lay beneath the desert sun. My father and I watched teams of men in monkey suits slowly tearing apart planes. Some of them wore welding masks, sparks shooting from their tools that made a sound worse – longer and higher pitched – than a human scream. I had to hold my ears and, at times, close my eyes as my father and I watched two men with a huge wrench, which they could only lift and manipulate together, pry the propeller from an old prop plane, place it on a dolly, and wheel it away. That propeller was taller than either man, and they had to work carefully and slowly to lower it. It was like a very large, prehistoric bone, a dead thing. I must have been eight or nine, just a kid, and didn't like that place at all – the noise and something else that I couldn't have put into words. It had nothing to do with my simple dream of being a pilot. Nonetheless, my father kept patting me on the back. 'Isn't this something?' he shouted over the racket. 'Isn't it?' I couldn't tell him that it frightened me. Adults don't understand the things that bother kids; and I knew I couldn't tell him how much I wanted to leave, how glad I was when we got in the car and drove away from that odd place. And because the Bone Yard was not the nicest thought to resort to as I drove through the Avenues that day with my mother, I tried to think of something else. I began to picture myself in an oxygen mask and goggles in the cockpit of a fighter jet. I was very careful about it, trying to see all the details – the unimaginably complex panel of switches, levers, and dials in front of me over which, as a military pilot, I would have complete understanding and mastery, of course. I'd be doing twenty Gs very easily, holding something like a large joystick between my legs and blasting right over the mountains. The snowy bald peaks rushed by below me as I left the Salt Lake valley behind, hurtling west at Mach speed, nothing but mountains and an empty, endless stretch of land in front of me. I crossed the deserts of Nevada, the Mohave, and Death Valley and knew I'd reached California as soon as I saw the peaks of the Sierras, which would take seconds to put behind me, doing three times the speed of sound, even though that probably wasn't humanly possible. To make it possible, I was wearing a special flight suit that combated G forces so that I could keep the air in my lungs, so that my circulation kept going, so that my brain got the oxygen it needed. I kept flying west like that until I came to the ocean, the whole world simplified by water wherever I looked. The sun was in front of me, of course, a red giant on which, at my altitude, I could see on its surface the firestorms I'd read about, great scarlet waves of hydrogen and other burning gases whipping up winds thousands of degrees centigrade. I'd seem to be flying between the blue earth and the red sun, then, and I'd just keep flying like that, between fire and water, not ever turning back. My jet was armed to the teeth with computerized bombs and heat-seeking missiles, with every destructive device that war jets could carry. I just held my course, looking down at my instruments now and then as I followed the sun. It would have been good to stay in that thought for a while, but I couldn't because I'd reached the edge of the world and it was going nowhere. There was nothing but space and light and water. That wasn't a place I could stay. So I opened my eyes – only then realizing that I had even closed them – and looked over at my mother. 'Please stop,' I said then. 'Please just pull over to the side of the road and talk to him.' I had the feeling that when we reached Curtis Smith's house everything would be decided. Everything would be finished.

'Just let me do things, Steven. Please. I don't want you to get involved in this.'

'Sure,' I said. 'I'll just pretend I'm not here. I'll do that, okay.'

'Stay out of it.'

'You've put me in it,' I said. 'You're the one who's taking us to meet your lover.' But she wasn't talking to me anymore. She just sat straight and kept driving up that hill. I wondered when we'd reach the top of it. I wondered how high up above the city rich people lived. I wondered how rich Curtis Smith was. I wondered what my father would do against him. Then I had this thought that sometimes helps me, this simple thought. *Whatever* is the thought. *Whatever.* One simple word. I'd just say it in my mind and sometimes it'd loosen the whole world up. *Whatever,* I thought. *What-goddamn-motherfucking-ever.* That was my thought, and it might have worked had I not remembered that my father had said the same word right after he had taken the fifty-dollar bill from my mother, which he shouldn't have done. It was a cowardly thing to do and a cowardly thing to say. So that thought was no help to me at all, especially now that we turned onto Mars Drive – no kidding – and then into this horseshoe driveway in front of what must have been Curtis Smith's house. 'This is it,' my mother said, parking behind two cars – a black Corvette and a red BMW – that sat quietly gleaming, wet from the rain and impossibly new looking.

I felt ashamed of our Buick, the rough, bestial growl of its engine, the oily stink of it, and started to understand why my mother was happy to leave it to my father, started to see that her decision had nothing to do with what a 'great find' my father had made when he bought the Buick. Jesus. We were all liars. My whole family was.

My father's cab stopped at the mouth of the driveway and, for a moment, I thought he might turn around and leave. Then, very slowly, the yellow car moved into the driveway. My father stepped out of it while it was still moving so that when he hit the ground he nearly fell and had to struggle to right himself.

'What's happening?' Jenny asked, her head popping above the lip of the backseat. Her eyes looked sleepy.

'We're here,' my mother said again.

Jenny turned, saw the house, and seemed to wake up immediately. 'Oh,' she said.

Right away when I looked at that house, I could have only one thought, a thought I did not like at all. Curtis Smith had stolen our dream. That house should have been ours, mine, my sister's, my father's and mother's. All of us together should have had that house. It was made of a natural wood, stained the deep, blond color of butterscotch. Its three stories supported two large balconies furnished with chairs, tables, and yellow sun umbrellas. I couldn't begin to count the windows, dark-tinted like sunglass lenses and full of a black reflective light even in the bluish air of early evening. The front yard leapt upward some twenty yards, broken only by a row of small trees and oval garden plots, padded with wood chips, that would flower in the spring, and landed at the front step before a set of polished, red-oak double doors with heavy, brass handles and a small window protected by a rake of cast-iron bars in the middle of one door. I kept expecting those doors to open. I kept expecting Curtis Smith to come out. But the house was absolutely quiet. My father was looking up at it. He couldn't seem to take his eyes off it. 'I understand,' he said. He walked slowly backwards, still looking at the house, taking more of it in. He stumbled into the wet dirt of a circular garden and came to a stop. 'Financially secure!' he shouted. If anyone was home inside that monstrous and beautiful house, they could hear my father. I thought I could feel them looking down at us through one of the dark windows. I wondered what my father looked like seen from up there. I wondered how clumsy and weak and desperate he would appear.

'Please don't shout like that, Billy,' my mother said. We had both stepped out of the car. When Jenny got out, my mother looked back at her and said, 'You get back in the car and wait for us. It won't be long.'

'Okay,' Jenny said.

But before she could sit back down, my father said, 'I want her to stay out here. I want to say something to all of you. I want Jenny to hear.'

Jenny looked at my mother for permission. She nodded. 'As long as you stop shouting,' she said. 'No more shouting. If you shout, she goes back in.'

'You're different,' my father said. He was looking at her

now with the same shocked expression he had had when looking at that house, as if she were just as unexpected, just as impossible to take in and understand. 'You're cold, absolutely cold.'

'Do you agree not to shout?' she asked.

'Okay,' he said. Jenny walked over to my mother.

'All right,' my mother said, 'what would you like to say to us?'

My father looked back up at the house. He didn't seem to know what to feel, and I knew then that he was stalling, that he had no plan, no way of remedying this situation, nothing to say, that he was hopeless, really, and was just trying to gain a few minutes. 'It's a beautiful house,' he finally said. I don't know why he had to say that. He wasn't speaking with bitterness or sarcasm. He laughed and shoved his hands deep into his pockets and nodded his head at that enormous house. 'I guess I come in last, don't I?' he asked.

'Maybe you should go, Billy,' she said.

'Am I supposed to apologize now, beg for forgiveness or something, so that we can all get back together? Is that what I'm supposed to do, Mary?' He was smiling, trying to act as though none of this mattered to him, as if his question were facetious. But his smile was thin, and he couldn't seem to keep it.

'No,' she said.

He looked down at himself and brushed off the front of his wet jeans, even though there was nothing on them. Then he began shivering. 'Jesus am I cold,' he said. He just stood there, holding himself.

'You should go home and change, Billy,' my mother said.

'I want to know what I'm supposed to do. What should I do, for Christ's sake, Mary?'

'You're shouting,' my mother said.

'I'm sorry,' my father said in a softer voice now. 'So tell me.'

'There's nothing to do. I don't want you to do anything. I just want you to go home now.'

My father sat down Indian style, the way a kid sits, in the wet dirt beneath him, and beat the ground once with his fist.

'We're not going to ask you in, Billy.'

My father looked up, and I saw that he wasn't angry with her, that he no longer had the strength to be angry with her. He was shaking his head and pulling his long wet hair back. He tried to hold her gaze, but he couldn't. He had to look back down. 'Is that right?' he asked.

'Yes,' she said.

We were all quiet for some time, and I looked behind me, because I no longer wanted to look at my father sitting like that on the ground, hugging himself. The section of the sky above the mountains was a glowing pink while another section of it was black with clouds. I faced them again. 'She was lying,' I said to him, because somebody needed to say something and because I was pretty sure what I was saying was the truth. 'She does too love you. She can't help loving you.'

My mother looked at me and I thought I saw anger in her eyes, but her voice wasn't angry when she said, 'That's not enough. It never changed things. Not in all the years we've been together it hasn't. I could go on loving him forever and it wouldn't do a thing.'

My father smiled at me. 'Thanks, Steven,' he said. 'Thanks for being on my side. Thanks for believing in me.' He looked behind him then at a blue-and-white Salt Lake City Police car that had just pulled onto Mars Drive from Milky Way Boulevard and quietly came to a stop, its motor still running, on the opposite side of the street from us. Its windows were tinted black and reflected a portion of Curtis Smith's front yard. 'I'll be damned,' my father said quietly, looking over his shoulder at the car. 'It looks like your rich friend called the cops on me.' He was worried enough to speak quietly now, too quietly for his voice to be heard by the cops inside that car. I looked at the house again, this time sure that we were being watched and that whoever was watching us had the law on his side and was a powerful person for that reason. 'I wish you would go in there and tell your friend not to do that. I am not a criminal, for Christ's sake.' He looked back at the cop car again and picked up a good-size rock out of the garden dirt beneath him, weighing it in his hand. 'I suppose that would be a stupid thing to do, wouldn't it?' my father said to himself.

'Yes, Billy,' my mother said. 'That would be a stupid thing to do.' He let the rock drop from his hand. 'Go now,' she said. She reached out to him with the keys to the Buick. 'You take the car,' she said.

'No!' he shouted. 'Hell, no!' The cop didn't like the sound of my father shouting because she — a lady cop — stood out of her car, walked around to the other side of it, the side closest to us, and leaned against it. She was blond and wore her hair inside her cop hat and had one of those belts with weapons on it. 'I am not a criminal,' my father whispered viciously. 'I am doing nothing wrong here. Nothing.'

'This yard doesn't belong to you, Billy,' my mother said in a soft voice. 'This is private property.' You could barely hear the cop's radio, the static and sounds of voices speaking out of it.

My father stood up, water dripping from his backside. 'I'm not feeling too well,' he said. In fact, he looked sick. His eyelids were purple, and his face was white. He looked too skinny and maybe hungry. 'So I'm going to leave. But I'm coming back. I'm not giving up.' He looked at Jenny. 'How's that watch, Jen-Jen?' he asked. 'You still like it?'

'Yes,' she said.

'What time is it, then?' he asked.

She looked at her watch, which she hadn't done for a while now. 'It's thirty-five minutes after six.' She smiled at him, but there was something stiff and formal between them.

'That's a very nice outfit,' he said, gesturing at my sister's new uniform. 'Does that mean you made the cheerleader squad?'

'No,' Jenny said, almost shyly. 'I'm on the drill team. I'm a Billmorette now.'

'Wonderful,' he said. 'Congratulations. That's really . . .' He couldn't finish his sentence. He looked at me and then at Jenny again, and then looked quickly over his shoulder at the lady cop, who was watching us. 'Does one of you want to come home with me?' he asked. Jenny held more tightly to our mother.

'They're going to stay with me for now,' our mother said.

'I'm just asking for one of them.'

'No, Billy,' my mother said.

'Steven can make his own decisions.' He looked at me. 'You're old enough to decide what you want to do.' He was confident that I would come with him. I could see that right away. But he looked so cold and unwell, and I glanced over at the cab and saw that scary driver moving behind the wheel to his music. I didn't want to get in that cab and I didn't want to be near my father, near his hopelessness, near his bone-cold chill, near his inability to stop what was happening that day.

'He's staying with me, Billy,' my mother said. She put her hand on my shoulder, and I felt her fingers trembling. But I also felt her strength, her determination to keep me.

'Don't,' I said. I shook my shoulder free and took a step away from her.

'Steven,' she said.

'He can decide for himself,' my father said. 'What do you say, Steven?' He looked at me.

'I don't know,' I said.

'What does "I don't know" mean?' he asked. 'What the hell does that mean?'

'Mom says I have to stay.' I looked up at her, and she put her hand out toward me again. But I moved another step away. I didn't want her to touch me. I really didn't. 'I'll be home later tonight. We'll all be home later tonight.'

'You're going with her?'

'I'm just staying a few more hours.'

'You're choosing to go with her?' He was shaking his head at me.

'I'm not choosing anything.'

'Jesus,' he said.

'Don't you do this to him, Billy,' my mother said.

'I'm not doing anything to anyone.' He looked at me and said nothing. He just nodded, as if I knew what that meant, before he turned around and went back to his cab.

I watched him as the cab drove off. I almost ran after him. I almost shouted at him to wait. I wanted to tell him that I had changed my mind, that I was going with him. Instead, I stood there and watched until the yellow car drove down the hill. When it disappeared, the lady cop got back in her car and my mother walked up behind me and put her hand on my back. 'Don't touch me, please,' I said.

She took her hand back and stepped away from me.

My mother was shaky after my father had left and needed

some time to just sit. So she made us all get back into the Buick and started the engine and ran the heater on high until we warmed up. A white mist covered the windows through which Curtis Smith's house slowly lost definition. You could just barely make out the cop car as it pulled away from the curb and drove down Mars Drive. 'Why was he looking at me like that?' I asked.

She was tapping her fingers on the steering wheel and thinking about something. 'He's just upset. He'll get over it.'

'He won't get over it,' I said.

'He'll get over it.'

'Why was he mad at me? I'm not the one he should be mad at.'

'I'm sorry,' she said then, though she didn't sound sorry. She sounded angry. 'I'm sorry if I've involved you too much in all this, okay?'

I looked out the window and let my mother know I was going to remain silent, which really pissed her off.

'Okay?' she said in a fierce whisper.

'Whatever,' I said. It was the right word to say this time. It was satisfying as hell to say, in fact.

My mother wiped the mist from the rearview mirror, looked at herself, and forgot all about whether or not I accepted her apology. 'I've ruined myself,' she said. 'I can't see anybody looking like this.' Her tears had melted her cosmetics away. She began cleaning her face off with Kleenex and handing me the bright, bruise-colored clumps of tissues, which I had no place to throw except on the wet mat at my feet, where they made a pulpy mush of color. She redrew her face, pausing to clear the fog from the mirror a few times. When she'd finished, she turned around to show Jenny and me. 'How do I look?' she asked.

'Okay,' Jenny said.

Our mother wiped a large peephole in the fogged window and looked out at the house. 'It's not why you like him?' I asked her. 'The house, I mean.'

'Does it have a pool?' Jenny asked. She was looking out at it, too.

'In the back,' she said. She looked over at me. 'No, Steven,' she said. 'That's not why.' She seemed to pause and think about her answer carefully. 'It's certainly not why. But I can't say it isn't important. The fact that he knows how to put his life together and keep it together is something to consider.'

I saw Jenny's face fall. She was looking down at her lap. 'Maybe I don't want to meet him now,' Jenny said.

My mother put her hand on Jenny's cheek. 'It will be okay,' she said. 'I promise.'

'It's not going to be okay,' I said.

She thought of something. 'He's a pilot,' she said. 'Curtis has a small plane. I'm sure he'd take you up in it.'

'I don't care if he has a stupid plane,' I said. 'I don't care what he has.'

'I just thought you might like to know.'

'I don't want to meet him,' Jenny said.

'You can stay in the car. How would that be?' My

mother knew exactly what she was doing, since any kind of isolation was the severest form of punishment to Jenny. She hated more than anything to be excluded and left alone.

'I don't know,' Jenny said.

'I'm not going,' I said. 'I'm staying with Jenny.'

'Okay,' my mother said. 'You stay in the car, then.' My mother stood up out of the Buick and slammed the door. For an instant, both Jenny and I watched her from our seats. Then Jenny burst out, not even bothering to close her door, and sprinted to my mother's side. I should have stayed in my seat. I should have sat right there. I should never have moved. But I was afraid of being left in that car. I was every bit as afraid of loneliness as Jenny was. I was afraid of losing our mother. And so I picked up my white garbage bag and zipped my coat, walked around to Jenny's door, locked and closed the goddamned thing, and followed them.

6

Curtis Smith's doorbell made the sound of an imperial gong. Jenny clung to our mother, their arms entwined. I hugged myself, cradling my arm in its sling, as if my injury were the most precious thing in the world to me, while a rain so fine and insubstantial that it hardly seemed to exist tickled my face and neck. 'His children's names are Andrea and Curtis Junior,' she whispered. 'They're staying at Curtis's house this week, so you'll be meeting them.'

'Don't expect me to be nice,' I said.

She reached over and squeezed my good shoulder firmly. 'I do expect you to be nice, Steven.' She looked at me for a moment, and I could tell that she was embarrassed or worried. 'Why don't you go put that garbage bag in the car, kiddo? I don't think you need to carry it around, do you?'

I looked down at it. I sure the hell wasn't going to give

it up. It gave me something to do with my good hand, for one thing. It gave me something to hold on to. 'I like it,' I said.

But there was no time for an argument because the door opened then, and a man shorter, fatter, older, and no better dressed than my father stood in the doorway. He had his kids – Andrea and Curtis Jr. – on either side of him. I could tell they were scared – all of them. The little kid, Curtis Jr., who had a soft, fat face with blue eyes and who was squirming beneath his father's arm, must have been five or so. Before anything was said, the boy started picking his nose, and Curtis took his son's hand and held it tightly. 'No,' Curtis said. The boy was dressed in these brown corduroy pants and a white oxford with one of those polo ponies on the chest – Ralph Lauren for little kids. The girl was taller – she might have been ten or so – and was staring down at her shiny-as-hell black shoes with a fine strap through which the pink of her stockings seemed to burn and give off light. She wore this dress that came down just below her knees and was the color and texture of cotton candy. She hated us. I could tell that without even seeing her face.

'Hi,' Curtis said to all of us. Nobody answered. Even my mother remained silent. Curtis looked at me, and I was shocked to recognize his eyes. Shallow and blue, they were his mother's, and I thought about how we each knew the other's mother, only he loved mine and I – or so I told myself – hated his. He was, as far as I could see, a slob. For one thing, both his children – probably thanks to his ex-wife – were better dressed than he. He wore blue jeans with the cuffs rolled up once over a pair of spit-shined cowboy boots, the brown leather textured like rattlesnake skin, and a shieldlike belt buckle with a chunk of turquoise in the middle. His arms were muscled, but his belly stretched the green fabric of his polo shirt a little. His hands were thick and short, like paws. In one, he still held his son's nose-picking hand while the other held the door open with powerful, stubby fingers. His thin blond hair was a burnished, reddish gold. His teeth were very white. 'Would you like to come in?' he asked.

'Thank you,' our mother said.

The ceilings in the house were so high that Jenny and I couldn't stop looking up. 'Wow,' Jenny said, 'this is big, huge.' She actually said that.

'Shush,' I said, even though it was too late to shut her up.

'Your mother's going to give you the tour later,' Curtis said. He hung my mother's and sister's coats on hooks in the hallway, helping them take them off in a gentlemanly way. I refused to let him take mine. We wouldn't be staying that long, I told him. Then he led us into the sitting room through a tiled entryway that clicked beneath my mother's shoes and squished, slippery, beneath my sneakers. There were balconies on the inside of that house, too. They extended out from the second and third floors into the airy height of the steepled ceiling, cut in places by long, rectangular windows through which you could see sections of blue evening sky.

Our two families sat in the living room on couches opposite one another. I put my sack of shitty clothes down between me and my mother and sister. Because she knew what was in the bag, Jenny scooted farther away from me and closer to my mother, which I didn't mind at all. That's when I really noticed that room and a particularly freaky thing about it. It was more or less the living room I pictured in my dream – the one where my family was playing chess and backgammon and acting completely civil. The couches were the same soft shade of white as the couches in my dream. Just as in my dream, the pulled curtains were white, the carpet and two sitting chairs were white, and a large window in front of us looked out on what my father had called the million-dollar view, a view of the Salt Lake Valley where a wet, blue evening had just fallen over a grid of bright dots, alive, circulating with light.

'Do you play?' he asked me. I was looking at this grand piano – also white, a hard, shellacked, celestial white – pushed to the back of the room.

'No,' my mother said, as if this fact embarrassed her, 'he doesn't.'

'Neither do I,' Curtis said. 'But my daughter does. We could get you lessons if you wanted.'

I didn't respond. Curtis's son was picking his nose again and this time, without saying anything, his father gently took the offending hand and held it.

'I guess Steven doesn't want to talk right now,' my mother said.

'I understand,' Curtis said. I wished he hadn't said that. *I understand*. Jesus. How could he have really meant that?

When he looked over at Jenny, she said right away, 'Hi, I'm Jenny.' She'd evidently decided to be as social as ever and to deny that anything terrible was happening. When she put her hand out, her skinny fingers were shaking, and we could all see that she was terrified.

Curtis smiled and reached across a glass-topped coffee table to shake her hand. 'Very nice to meet you, Jenny.'

Then she went on to Curtis Smith's kids. 'Hi,' she said to the little girl, who wouldn't even look at her until Curtis said 'Andrea' in this disciplinarian tone, and she finally met my sister's gaze with her chubby face.

'Hi,' Andrea said, though she wouldn't shake my sister's hand, and Jenny had to move on to the little boy who, when she addressed him, buried his face in his father's side.

'Jenny is very sociable,' my mother said, laughing awkwardly. 'She really likes people.'

'I wish I could say the same for mine,' Curtis said.

'She can be a real jackass, is what she can be,' I said.

'All right, Steven,' my mother said.

Curtis looked at my mother for a long moment without saying anything. 'It's been raining all day,' he finally said.

'Yes,' she said. Her face was chilly and still.

'I'm glad you came, Mary,' he said. I knew — by the way he'd said that and by the way he couldn't seem to stop looking at her — that he must have had to convince her to come, that he'd had to ask more than once, that the decision hadn't been easy for her and still wasn't, and that more than anything in the world right then Curtis Smith wanted my mother to stay. 'I really am glad you came.' You could hear it in his voice – how glad he was, how much he loved her, just as she'd said he did. She smiled at him – God, did I wish she hadn't smiled – and he smiled back, and they held each other's gazes for a long time and in a way that made me feel sick, though I was empty, hollow. I could neither throw up nor shit my pants. I could only sit there and be sick.

'What's wrong with him?' little Curtis asked, staring at me.

'Well,' my mother said, laughing very inappropriately, considering what she said next, 'somebody hurt him, I'm afraid.'

'Oh,' the kid said, still looking at me.

Curtis Smith's daughter stood up from the couch, walked over to a side window, lifted the white curtain, and peered out. 'You don't just stand up like that in the middle of a conversation, Andrea,' Curtis Smith said.

'Who was that man on our lawn?' Andrea asked, still peering out the window.

I saw my mother glance at Curtis Smith. 'That was my father,' I said.

'Come back over here and sit down,' Curtis said.

Andrea didn't move from the window. She turned around and looked at me as if she were trying to see the resemblance between me and the man who had been shouting on her lawn. 'Is he going to come back?' she asked. 'I don't want him to come back.' Little Curtis was staring at me again with these large, dopey, frightened eyes.

'Stop staring at me,' I said.

'Steven,' my mother said.

'Is he?' Andrea asked again. 'Is he going to come back?'

'No, Andrea,' my mother said.

'Yes, he is,' I said, looking right at Curtis Smith. 'He said he was coming back.'

'When is he coming back?' Andrea asked.

'Nobody is coming back,' Curtis Smith said.

'I think he is,' Andrea said.

'He promised he would,' I said.

'See,' Andrea said.

'Enough, Steven,' my mother said.

'What's he have in his bag?' Little Curtis was pointing at it.

'Stuff,' I said.

'I want you to stop looking out that window, Andrea,' Curtis said. 'Why don't you play us a song on the piano?'

'I don't want to play the piano,' she said.

'One song,' he said. 'It'll make you feel better.'

She walked over to the instrument, sat down, and started playing this lush rendition of that old love song 'The Rose' – all the girls in my junior high school in Boise had known it and sung it to each other on the bus – about rivers and thorns and flowing waters and how love is a rose, a very beautiful rose that has thorns. I was surprised by her skill, by the fact that she played without looking at her hands, her eyes closed and her small, pudgy body fluid and loose in that pink cotton-candy dress, as she worked the pedals with her feet and sang in this surprisingly big, womanly voice – a voice you wouldn't expect a ten-year-old girl to have – until she all at once stopped playing and said, 'I think he's going to come back. I do.' She seemed about to cry.

My mother lost it then. 'He is not coming back!' she half shouted. Andrea ran across the room and curled into her father, who looked ridiculous because he was actually smiling, straining to pretend that everything was as it should be. 'I'm sorry,' my mother said to Andrea.

After that, we ran out of things to say for what felt like ten minutes. My mother cleared her throat, folded her arms, and unfolded them. Curtis fisted up a hand and kneaded it into his thigh until his knuckles cracked. His son was pulling on a button on the couch cushion and yawned without covering his mouth. 'Well,' Curtis finally said, 'this is difficult for all of us, I know. I'm a little nervous myself.' When nobody said anything, he tried again. 'It's great for all of us to meet.'

'Yes,' my mother said. 'It is.'

'What's that a picture of?' Jenny asked Curtis Smith. She was pointing to a photograph sitting next to me on a mahogany side table.

'That's me in front of my airplane,' he said. In the photograph, Curtis Smith was dressed in a flight suit, holding a crash helmet and standing in front of a small plane, which I happened to know was a P-51 Mustang;

I'd built and painted a plastic model of that plane a few years before. 'The P-51 was the best fighter we had in the Second World War,' he said. 'A great war plane.' Something about Curtis Smith was surprising me. I hated the fact that he didn't look like a successful lawyer. I'd wanted him to be some rich man's shadow, some guy with a mirrored cigarette holder and an English accent. I'd wanted him to be a real asshole and not this squat, thick man who wore blue jeans and who might just be nice, as my mother had said. He was shaking his head, admiring his photograph before he put it down. 'I get a little carried away with planes. I sometimes think I should have gone into aeronautics. You have any interest in flying, Steven?' he asked. He was trying to be suave and conversational now, threading his fingers together and pressing both hands against his knee, which had begun to motor up and down. 'If you'd like to go up some time, we could do that. It scares Curtis here a little. He's not really ready for it yet, are you?' He gave the kid this very affectionate hug, pulling him in close because he was clearly afraid, though not at the moment, of planes.

'Steven's quite interested in flying,' my mother said. 'He used to build model airplanes and paint them all the time. Didn't you, Steven?'

'Would you please shut up,' I said.

She grabbed a lock of hair at the back of my head and tugged. 'You watch yourself,' she said.

Curtis turned around then and asked his kids to leave the room, to go down to the TV room for a while. 'I'd like to talk to Jenny and Steven for a minute,' he told them.

'Why?' Andrea asked. 'I don't want to leave.'

'I'm afraid you're going to have to, honey,' he said. He clearly knew how to lay down the law with his kids because she didn't ask again. She got up and took her little brother by the hand, and they walked out of the room and left us alone with Curtis.

'I want to assure you of a few things,' he said, turning back to us. He cleared his throat and looked at my sister and then at me. 'You're both old enough to understand, and so I thought maybe you'd like to know something.' I had no idea what he was about to say and it half scared me. 'Your mother won't be staying here at first. She'll be staying at my sister's until things get settled. You understand?' I didn't, but I didn't say anything. He explained that his sister lived just down the hill, that she was a very nice person, that her family would welcome my mother. 'Mary will be here during the day. She'll be here for meals, for breakfast and lunch and dinner. Later,' he said, pausing, looking at my mother and smiling, then looking back down at us, 'later, when things are more set, she'll be here more' – he was looking for a word – 'permanently. We thought that, being a little older and understanding the situation, you might like to know that.'

I still didn't understand. I looked over my shoulder at my mother, who was blushing, ashamed as hell. 'Please don't tell me anymore,' I said. 'It's none of my business. I don't want to know it.'

Curtis's knee began motoring up and down again. For such a thick-bodied man, he was an emotional weakling. Both he and my father had that in common. 'I'm sorry,' he said. 'I thought you might appreciate' – he stumbled on the word – 'understand – the morality of it.'

'No,' I said. 'I don't understand anything.'

Because he couldn't look at me anymore, he looked at my mother. 'Maybe you should show them around the house now, Mary.'

We followed our mother up a flight of polished stone steps, the open space of the first floor yawning beneath us. It was still drizzling outside. Tiny beads of rain accumulated on the black rectangular skylights in the ceiling above. The second floor was a balcony that circled the entire house, leading at both ends to staircases. A little white box on the wall flashed a red light at us as we passed. 'What's that?' Jenny asked.

'That's a motion detector,' my mother said. 'It's part of the security system.'

The air of that house smelled of Windex, of clean glass and cold, freshly scrubbed porcelain. 'It's not comfortable,' I said. 'It's too damn big.'

'I like it okay,' Jenny said. 'Can we see Andrea's and Curtis's bedrooms?'

'We can peek in,' my mother said.

Little Curtis's room had a walk-in closet about the size of our rooms at home, a glass door leading out to a balcony, an attached bathroom with a tub the shape and size of a whirlpool, and a large mirror above the copper basin of the sink. He had Mickey Mouse stuff all over the place – Mickey Mouse sheets, a Mickey Mouse alarm clock and a set of ears on his dresser, a poster on his wall of Mickey and Minnie Mouse hugging each other, pressing their mouse ears together and knotting their mouse tails up in this very loving way. Andrea's room was the same as little Curtis's – with a bathroom and balcony and large walk-in closet – only it was all pink, pink walls, carpet, and bedding. Right away Jenny started touching stuff. 'Andrea's bed has a canopy,' she said, letting her hand sink into one of the large pink pillows. She turned the closet light on, walked in, and came out with a bright red dress. 'How many dresses does she get to have?' Jenny asked no one in particular. She was just looking at that dress in her hand, studying it.

'That's not your dress,' I said, because she needed to hear that. 'Put it back. Tell her to put it back,' I said to my mother, who had wandered into Andrea's bathroom.

I picked up a pink cordless telephone on the bedside table, turned it on, and listened to the dial tone. 'She has her own stupid pink telephone,' I said, surprised that it was real, more than just a toy. 'She's only ten.' I was listening to the dial tone, still amazed.

'That's not yours,' Jenny said, mimicking me. 'Put it back.'

'I know that,' I said. 'Don't you think I know that?'

'Come look at this,' our mother said, calling us to the bathroom door. She was sitting on the edge of Andrea's huge oval bathtub, water running from the brass faucet as she passed her fingers through the stream. She lifted her hand and showed us the water dripping from her fingertips, as if to prove the reality of it. Jenny walked over to the copper sink, turned the water on, and touched with her fingers – as if she, too, could not quite believe it – a bar of soap in a marble dish. Looking at herself in the mirror above the sink, she started washing her hands.

'That's not your soap,' I said.

'This towel is so soft,' she said, drying herself now.

Jenny walked out of the bathroom then, through a sliding glass window, and onto the balcony – also not hers – that overlooked the backyard. 'The yard is huge,' she said. 'Huge.' She was standing out there in the drizzle, looking down on an expanse of grass lit by these little lamps sunk at intervals into the ground. She filled her lungs slowly with air. Above her, an umbrella of yellow light spread and turned the tiny beads of rain to flecks of gold. Below, the pool was uncovered and also lit – a strange, otherworldly slab of glowing blue from which steam as thick as rags rose into the wet air. I stood out there beside her now in the bright rain, looking over the yard and picturing something I shouldn't have been picturing, seeing it almost as if it were real – Noir out there running, devouring all that space, leaning into the ground and a little sideways the way he does when he really sprints, his tongue dangling out of the side of his mouth and his eyes focused and dark. That was a terrible thought and I tried to put it out of my mind. He'd have loved it, though. No more hours tangled in his chain. He really would have loved it.

'It's nice, isn't it?' my mother's voice asked from behind us.

'It's a stupid outdoor pool,' I said, remembering that none of this was ours, remembering that what we wanted was an indoor pool just off the living room. 'An outdoor pool is no good in the winter.'

'He keeps it heated in the winter,' she said. 'He says it can be nice to take a swim in the snow. You could even swim in the rain. You could swim right now, if you wanted.'

'I don't want to,' I said.

Just then, as if to prove her point, Andrea, little Curtis, and Curtis walked outside in their swimsuits. They were all plump, white, and very pale in the electric glow of the lamps. Curtis carried little Curtis, who was sucking his thumb.

'Hi,' Jenny said, waving down at them.

Little Curtis saw us first. 'Why are they standing on Andrea's balcony?' he asked. He got mad or scared. 'Get off her balcony!' he shouted.

'Curtis,' Curtis Smith said.

My mother stepped out then. 'I'm sorry,' she said. 'I thought I'd show them around before I took them to their rooms.' I couldn't believe she had said that, actually shouted it. Our rooms. What the hell did that mean?

'Great,' Curtis said. 'Go right ahead. Then come down and join us, if you like.' He waved up at us.

'They don't have rooms here,' little Curtis said, looking at his father. 'Do they?'

Curtis Smith didn't know what to say, and neither did my mother. 'I'm sorry,' she said again.

Andrea, who had run on ahead of her father and little brother and had been about to jump in the pool, turned around then and saw all three of us standing on her balcony. 'They're in my room!' she shouted. 'Why are they in my room?' Then she looked right at me. 'He's got my telephone.' I looked down and noticed that I still had her pink cordless phone in my hand. She began bawling. 'Tell them to get out of my room! Out! Out!'

'Jesus,' my mother whispered.

She pulled Jenny in and then came out for me, tugging on my shoulder. Only I didn't move. I looked down at that screaming girl and her father, who was saying, 'Shush, shush, you be nice, Andrea. You calm down.' I didn't know why Curtis Smith was telling her to calm down since I understood Andrea completely. I understood that she felt – and should have felt – completely violated by us. I understood that we had trespassed. I understood that a little girl living in a fortress like that with motion detectors, an alarm system, heavy doors with deadbolt locks, telephones in every room, a girl who had a lawyer for a father and lots of money and two new cars in her horseshoe driveway and a large pool heated during the winter was used to feeling safe and was probably getting one of her first real lessons in fear from me. I didn't mind that at all. I just stared her down while she screamed at me. I let her know that I was trespassing, that I knew it, and didn't give a damn. I let her know that she should be terrified of me, that she had every reason to be. I stood there like that until she couldn't scream anymore, until she ran up to her father and hid her wet face in his belly, and until my mother finally grabbed the back of my neck and said, 'God help you if you don't get inside this minute.'

Out in the hallway, my mother was pacing. Jenny and I looked over the railing onto the expansive first floor – the kitchen, the dining room, the entryway into the living room. 'Maybe,' my mother said. 'I don't know. I don't know.'

'What don't you know?' I asked.

'Maybe we should go,' she said. 'Maybe this arrangement isn't going to work.'

I stood away from the railing and looked at her. She was hugging herself with both arms as she paced. She stopped, took a cigarette out of her purse, and was about to light it. 'Oh, Christ,' she said then, and broke the cigarette in her hand and stuffed it back into her purse. 'No more smoking. Curtis doesn't want me to smoke.' She laughed. 'How long have I been trying to quit smoking?' she asked me.

'A long time,' I said.

'I don't follow through with things, do I?' she asked.

I didn't know why she was asking that. It seemed like a dangerous question to answer one way or the other. 'I think we should go,' I said.

mother and sister stood with their eyes closed, holding on to one another, and where I stood apart from them, leaning against the railing with my bad arm in a sling and my good arm holding my bag of shitty clothes. I felt far away from them then, as far away from them as I can ever remember feeling, and maybe that's why I did something I'd thought I'd never do. I looked up at the ceiling and into the black glass of the skylight, in which I could see the first floor reflected in a broken, unrecognizable way, and I prayed. I don't remember the words of my prayer, though I do remember how odd the word *God* felt in my mind, how odd that word was when you used it as a name, when you called out with it. No doubt I said other words, as well. No doubt I asked God to help me know what I could do to change the course of that day. Because that's all I wanted. I wanted the strength to know what I needed to do and I wanted the strength to do it. But the one thing I remember was the name of God and how, after saying it, nothing came back to me, no voice, no words, no whisper or sign, no feeling or sense or idea, nothing, just as earlier that day my sister and the bum with the beautiful voice had gotten no reply to their prayers. And I had to wonder how that Mormon kid, that missionary, no more than two years my senior, could have said that God spoke to him and would have spoken to us if we'd keep our hearts open. I had to wonder if I had a closed heart, an unapproachable and Godless heart, a heart of stone so that when I spoke the name of God in the dark of my mind I got nothing in return but silence. The missionary had lied to us, I decided. And his lie was as wrong as anything my family or I had done or ever would do.

'What do we want?' my mother said, though she wasn't really asking this question to me or Jenny or anyone. She was just saying those words out loud with her eyes closed.

'I want to go home,' I said quietly. 'Please.'

My mother opened her eyes and looked at Jenny. 'What do you want?'

'I don't know,' she said.

'You want to go home, don't you?' I said. 'Don't you?'

'Don't look at me like that,' Jenny said. She saw the threat in my eyes. 'Tell him to stop looking at me like that.'

'Steven,' my mother said, 'leave your sister alone.' Then she looked down at Jenny again. 'Do you want to go home or do you want to try and stay here for a while?'

'I don't know,' Jenny said. 'Don't ask me. Please don't.'

'Okay,' my mother said.

Jenny looked down at her purple Swatch, though she didn't say the time. She was thinking about our father, about the fact that he had bought her that stupid watch, that he had spent money we had not had on it, that he would do damn near anything for her. I knew she was, and so, it seemed, did my mother. 'You know that you'll be able to see your father whenever you want, even if we do stay here. You understand that, don't you?'

'I don't want to think about it,' Jenny said. 'Please let's not think about it. Please.'

'I think we need to think about it,' I said.

'No,' Jenny said.

'Leave her alone,' my mother said. She let go of Jenny and took another cigarette out, but then put it back in her purse. 'Curtis wants me to quit smoking,' she said. 'He cares about that. Your father never cared one way or the other.'

'That's not true,' I said, though I knew that it was true.

She looked down at herself. 'I'll probably get fat if I quit. But at least he cares if I'm healthy.' Then she looked at both of us, sighed, and said, 'Would you like to see your rooms now?'

'No,' I said.

'Maybe,' Jenny said.

'I'm going to the fucking car,' I said.

My mother dug the keys to the Buick out of her purse and plopped them in my hands. 'You can come back in,' she said, 'whenever you're ready.'

'I'll wait for you in the car,' I said.

I'd gotten halfway down the staircase before I stopped, giving my mother a chance to call me back, to say something that would stop me from leaving. But she didn't. So I turned around and hurried after them.

'It's so soft,' Jenny said, falling backwards into the lavender bedding. Lavender was her favorite color. The carpet and wallpaper were also lavender. It was clear that they had prepared the room for her. 'Soft, soft, soft,' Jenny said. 'It doesn't have a canopy like Andrea's. Do you think we could get a canopy?'

'We'll see,' my mother said.

Jenny shot up from her bed, walked over to the sliding glass door that led out to the balcony, and flipped the light switch on and off. 'I have my own balcony light,' she said. 'Look.' The darkness outside her window flashed with light. Then she slid the door open and closed, open and closed. 'This is my balcony door, isn't it?' She walked out onto the balcony and looked over the backyard again. Curtis and his kids had gone back inside. We could hear them down in the kitchen making a racket. 'They can't tell me to get off my balcony, can they?' she asked. For some reason, Jenny had started doing jumping jacks out on her balcony.

My mother smiled then and said, 'Your room is next door, if you'd like to take a look.'

'I'm not interested,' I said.

'It's just down the hallway.' I looked over my shoulder in that direction. 'Go ahead,' she said.

I shouldn't have, but I did. I walked down the hallway and opened the door – my door to my room – and looked in. It was the same as the others except for the russet brown carpet and the bedding – a down comforter and sheets that had all sorts of airplanes on them – biplanes, prop planes, fighter jets, the Concorde, the Boeing 747. Those sheets made me feel ashamed for ever having dreamed so stupidly of being a pilot, for ever having labored as a kid over model airplanes, for ever having uncapped tubes of epoxy, sorted through the little plastic parts – the wings, the rudder, the fuselage, the cockpit, the propellers – before gluing them and scraping the excess glue from the seams with an edge of cardboard, my finger-tips hardening, red and irritated, with that harsh adhesive, then applying tape, carefully painting, finally soaking the decals of stars and American flags in water and applying the fragile skins to the painted plastic. I had never flown, never been up in a plane. Our family had rarely taken trips. And when we did, we drove. Maybe that's why I stood there over those silly bedsheets – too young, I thought, for a fifteen-year-old boy, too stupid, insulting to my intelligence, I felt – and nonetheless wondered what it might be like to sit behind Curtis Smith in his vintage P-51 with a flight suit on and a crash helmet while we looked down on the curvature of the Earth below, the geometric cut of fields and farmland, the ground as seen from the air, a view I had only had from a TV screen or from my dreams before, the ripple of mountains on all sides, the city reduced to a mere texture of buildings and streets from which you could never distinguish your tiny house, even if it was a mansion like Curtis's. To the west and south beyond the city, where a desert as white as moonscape went on forever, you'd see the smooth expanse of the Great Salt Lake stretching like sheet metal for miles and the great iron-ore crater of the Kennecott Copper Mine gouged into the mountainside. It would all look perfect, sculpted and polished. I don't know why I saw it all so vividly – myself and Curtis way the hell up there with sunlight beading through the cockpit. That strange man's face — his eyes concealed in a dark aviation visor to protect them from the rays — glowed in a hard, clean light, the sort of light, I imagined, that you only got at ten or fifteen thousand feet. I had no doubt that he was a good pilot. I even had no doubt — seeing the way he'd hugged his frightened kid and gently prevented him from picking his nose in front of us — that he was, as my mother had said, a good man. I hoped I was wrong. All the same, I imagined him piloting that plane, looking over at me in this platinum, high-elevation light, and giving me the thumbs-up sign, the way pilots supposedly do, to which I gave him the same sign back. Everything's A-okay, it meant. Sometimes you can't help imagining things. Sometimes things just flash through your head, like that thought about Curtis and me in his plane. It depressed me, though, and after it was gone, I walked over to a desk made of a thick, blond hardwood. I leaned against it and pressed on it with my full weight, surprised by its solidity. My desk, I thought. Those words just came to me, too. I don't know why. They made me feel dark and greedy and somehow more powerful. I put my white garbage bag on top of my desk and then picked up a cordless phone. My phone, I thought as I listened to the dial tone. That felt good, so I thought it again. My phone. I had never had a phone before, not even the crappy kind with a cord. Then I walked over to the sliding glass door where I couldn't help mimicking my little sister, turning the balcony light on and off, and thinking, My balcony light. My balcony light. Only when I turned it off, I saw my bony, white

It was a Book of Mormon. I picked the book up and opened it to the first page, where it said, 'This Holy Book Belongs To'. My name had been written in the space below those words in somebody's careful handwriting. 'Who the hell wrote my name here?'

'That's a gift from Curtis,' she said.

'Jesus,' I said. 'He's Mormon. He's a stupid Mormon.'

'Keep your voice down, Steven,' she said. She was worried about Curtis hearing me, I knew. We could still hear them downstairs. It was a cavernous house in which voices traveled easily.

'That means that you're going to become a Mormon, too.' She didn't say anything. 'But we don't believe in God,' I said. 'We're atheists, aren't we?'

'That's your dad,' she said. 'I never said that. I'd like to believe in God, if I could. I told Curtis I'd try. That's all I promised him.'

'Christ.' I was beginning to understand the little talk about morality Curtis had just given us. 'That's why he won't have you stay here,' I said. I was beginning to understand why he was so damn nice, just as Janet Spencer and her parents were nice, according to my sister. I was beginning to understand why he didn't yell or argue, why he hugged his kids, why he nodded and smiled at me, why he didn't do anything but be nice and pleasant as can be.

'He didn't insist that I believe,' my mother said. 'He said he'd understand if I didn't see everything the way he sees it. We're determined to make that work.'

'Jesus Christ!' I shouted.

'Steven,' my mother said, pointing her finger at me. 'You should know that Curtis doesn't appreciate swearing. This is his house.'

'What's happening?' Jenny asked. She'd walked in my room with this thick purple bathroom towel – her towel – folded over her arm.

'He's a stupid Mormon,' I said, shaking the book in her face.

'What's wrong with that?' my sister asked.

I threw the book across the room and looked at my mother. 'You swear all the time, Mom,' I said. 'We all swear. Our family swears.' This was true. Even Jenny – who liked to act innocent as hell – got away with an occasional *shit* or *damn,* though she didn't often speak like this since she knew it wasn't girlish. 'Jenny swears,' I said, pointing at her.

'I do not,' she said.

'You do, too. You swear whenever you want. Nobody ever told you never to swear. And Mom swears. Doesn't she?' I asked Jenny.

'I don't know,' Jenny said.

My mother was looking down at her hands as if they were dirty or something. 'I guess I don't swear anymore,' she said. 'That shouldn't be too difficult to change. If I can quit smoking, I can do that, can't I?'

I could hardly recognize my mother then – this woman in new clothes and makeup who was going to try to believe in God and was determined to give up foul language forever. 'You're both liars,' I said. 'You're both full of shit. We swear!' I shouted. 'Fuck! Shit! Damn!' I was yelling and could hear my words fill the common area of the house.

'Steven Parker!' my mother shouted. She took a swipe at my face with her hand, but missed.

'Fuck! Fuck! Fuck!' I shouted. The second time she tried, she slapped me square across the mouth, slapped me so hard that I was quiet for a second and took a step backwards. The hot sting was amazing, and I put my hand to my mouth to cool it.

'Shut up!' she yelled at me. She looked furious. As far as I could tell, she hated me. That stupid bat was behind me, so I picked it up and swung it wildly. I saw her grab her hand.

'Jesus,' she whispered, holding on to herself.

'You hit her,' Jenny said. My sister had backed into a corner and was staring at me.

I didn't know what to do. I put the bat down, stepped away from it, then picked it up again, and took out the bedside lamp – *my* goddamn bedside lamp – its blue ceramic belly shattering, its bulb exploding. I turned and knocked *my* desk lamp from *my* desk, then smacked *my* cordless phone across the room and pulverized a small plant on my desk, terra-cotta shards and dirt falling to the carpet. Jenny ran out of the room, and I turned on *my* bed and began pounding away at that stupid comforter, at the airplanes all over it, pounding and pounding, until goose down floated in the air and rained slowly down as if time had almost come to a stop. I was swearing up a storm, shouting every word and phrase I knew – buttfuck, pigass, bitchfucker, asswipe – letting these combinations of words come out of me because we were the Parkers, and that's how we talked, that's who we were – the motherfucking, bitchassed, shitheaded Parkers. I kept on shouting like that until I felt someone's powerful arms bear hug me from behind. The bat dropped to the floor. I knew it was Curtis Smith. No one else in that house had that kind of strength. I felt his warm breath against my neck. 'Steven,' he said, 'you quiet yourself.'

'Fuck you!' Then: 'You're hurting my shoulder, you asshole!' I screamed until he let me go. But when I grabbed the bat again, he locked me in another bear hug.

'What did he do?' Andrea asked, peeking into my room. Her frightened little brother peeked his head in, too.

'Get out of my goddamn room!' I shouted at them. They both ran down the hall, and I really let Curtis Smith have it. I called him every name in the book until he lifted me up and squeezed the air out of me. The ceiling tilted oddly. I heard my breathing turn to a wheezing.

'Quiet,' he said in this gentle voice. 'You quiet yourself.'

My eyes watered and I could no longer make the words come out. It was silent, and in that silence both Curtis and I could hear the crisp shattering of glass, after which, warm and fast, Colonel Warner's urine soaked through my coat and dripped on Curtis Smith below me. That was strange. That even scared me. God didn't exist. God didn't answer when you called his name. God had no voice. God was a lie. Anyone who'd seen old Colonel Warner on his table would have known that. That old man was in darkness now and a small remaining part of him was spilling out into nothing.

'Jesus!' Curtis Smith shouted. He dropped me on the bed and looked at his arm, glistening with two trails of urine, though he didn't know that and he was probably very scared. His forearm had been nicked by the broken glass and a fine streak of blood – crimson and surprising – formed in an instant. He probably thought he was disintegrating or self-destructing. 'Jesus Christ!' he shouted.

I didn't want to be bad. I was tired of it already. All the same, it was worth it if only to hear that good man whom my mother thought she loved swear like that in his own fucking house.

7

I didn't remember falling asleep or even waking. I just remembered being awake – the sudden violence of sunlight, a hard, yellow pool that stung my eyes and made every dust mote in the air swirl. I blinked and tried to remember a dream – something about Noir whining, about my father walking naked in the street. Why was he naked? He hadn't seemed to know he was naked. His hair was wet, plastered to his head, and he hadn't shaved for days. I wanted to tell him that he needed to go inside or dress or do something. But for some reason, he couldn't hear me and just kept walking barefoot in the street through puddles as cars rushed by. I stopped thinking about that. It was just a stupid dream. I looked around the room, but recognized nothing. My sling was no longer on. It lay over the bed next to me with my red jacket in a tangle of ripped sheets and feathers. The room looked as if a flock of birds had just been slaughtered in it. I sat up and strained to remember. When I saw the white garbage bag on top of a desk, everything returned to me – Colonel Warner, shitting myself, Nurse Brown, Jenny hating me for what I had done to Mrs. Smith, my mother and Curtis cleaning up the shards of glass, clearing away the things that I had destroyed as I lay over the bed with my face in a pillow, refusing to speak to them until finally they closed the door behind them and left me. God, was that unpleasant to remember. I looked outside, squinting into the sun. A light snow fell despite the fact that I could see no clouds. Outside on the balcony, the wind was bitter, and I hurried back inside. A digital clock on the bedside table said 4:34 P.M. I'd slept through the entire day. No one had woken me. The day had passed, and no one had said anything. I wondered what had happened without me. I wondered what had changed that I could now do nothing about. I zipped my coat up and took my garbage bag from the desk and left that room.

Out in the hallway, I heard the front door slam, and from a second-floor window, I saw Curtis and my mother outside in the driveway where the Buick, its windshield silvered with frost, was still parked behind the Corvette and the red BMW. I hadn't expected to see the yellow cab out there, too, idling in the cold, with Noir – my good, stupid dog – in the backseat. Noir was sticking his white muzzle up against the slightly cracked window and sucking at the fresh air. No doubt the driver – a bald guy smoking a cigarette as he sat behind the wheel – hated Noir, and I was worried about him, since Noir was overfriendly and would beg for affection from anyone. But I was even more aware that the cab's presence meant that my father was here somewhere. My mother and Curtis were bundled up in winter coats of the same bright, banana yellow, his and hers winter coats, I guessed. My mother was looking down and to her side, anywhere but at Curtis, who was looking at her as he talked. He kicked one of his feet lightly at the concrete. I couldn't guess what he'd said to her that made her so suddenly close her eyes and shake her head and put her hands over her ears, the way Jenny so often did when she didn't want to hear something. 'Stop,' I said to the glass in front of me. 'Stop.' I wanted to protect her from whatever had made her do that. But I wasn't out there, of course. Curtis was, and he reached out to her then and touched her. He touched her shoulder, and she pushed his arm away and took a step back. Then he reached out to her again. This time she came to him and they held each other. I didn't want to look at that, but I did. The sun was out and the sky was this brilliant color of blue, so that you could see everything, you could even see the tiny crystals of ice in the air, a sign that, sun or no sun, it was brutally cold. I watched them holding each other for as long as I could, white breath smoking from their mouths. I didn't know what that meant, except that something was wrong. I rushed down the stairs and would have gone outside had I not seen my father's gray winter coat – slack and shapeless with too much wear – on a coat hook in the entryway. I found him in the white living room sitting on the couch opposite my little sister, though they weren't talking. Their backs to me, they were both staring out that huge window at the city below. My father didn't look like himself because he was wearing a dark blue suit, something I had never seen him wear before that afternoon. I didn't say anything for a long time. I just stood at the far end of the living room watching them stare through that window. 'Hi,' I said.

Jenny jumped in her seat a little. 'Oh,' my father said, turning around to look at me, 'it's you.' His face was very pale, and he was squinting at me and had to shield his eyes with his hand. 'Could you stand out of the sun, kiddo? I can't even look at you.' When I stepped forward, he put his hand down and said, 'That's better. Thank you.' But he didn't look at me for long. He looked down at the glass of ice water in his hand. 'It's a very nice glass,' he said. He lifted it up and we all stared at it for a moment – a beveled, crystal water glass. 'It's heavy. I was just telling your sister that you can tell quality glass from the weight of it.'

'You look good,' I said. 'In your suit and everything.' He didn't look good, though. The suit was too big for him. It hung on his shoulders and he looked small inside it. You could tell he wasn't used to wearing clothes like that because he didn't seem to know how to sit or hold himself or even what to do with his legs, which he just then crossed and uncrossed. He had on his best pair of dress shoes, which were scuffed down to the leather in places. He was clean-shaved and washed, but had nicked himself on his chin and cheek, where two tender raspberry marks showed. I could tell that he was nervous, that he was anxious about his appearance, that he was maybe even worried about how I saw him that day.

'I've felt better,' he said. 'I've felt much better.'

He put his water glass down on the glass tabletop, and I couldn't help but say, 'You're supposed to put it on the coaster.' I pointed at the coaster.

'Of course,' he said, picking the glass up again. 'When you have nice things . . .' But he didn't finish that thought. He looked over at the white piano. 'That's some instrument, isn't it? That's pretty fancy. A white piano. I thought pianos were supposed to be black.' He looked at me again. 'Last night was real quiet without you and Jenny.' He shook his head. 'I hadn't expected things to be so quiet.'

'I didn't think we were going to stay here. I thought we were going to leave after a while. If we'd known, Jenny and I would have gone with you.' I wanted Jenny to say something, to reassure him that what I'd said was true. But she just sat there looking down at her lap. She wore this very nice pair of tan pants and a blouse the soft white color of that living room. They were new, very expensive clothes. I was sure of that.

He smiled at me. I didn't understand why he would smile. I didn't know what that was supposed to mean. 'I would have made the same choice, kiddo,' he said.

'I didn't make any choice.'

'Sure you didn't,' he said.

'I didn't want to stay here,' I said. 'I didn't. I didn't.'

'Okay,' he said. 'Okay.'

'You don't believe me.'

'All right, Steven.' He raised his voice. 'I believe you.' But he didn't. He took a drink of his water. 'Your mom tells me you caused quite a ruckus over here last night.'

'What?' I said. 'What did she tell you?'

He waved his hand in the air, as if none of what she'd said to him mattered at all. 'Nothing,' he said.

'Are we going to go home now – you and me and Jenny and Mom?'

He looked down at himself and laughed. 'I thought these people would dress. I thought he'd have something like this on. I guess it looks as if your dad is trying too hard.' He pulled at his suit. He wore a dark blue tie with a mother of pearl tiepin in it. 'He's wearing blue jeans, for Christ's sake.'

'You look good,' I said again. 'Are you going to fight?' I asked.

'Pardon me?' he said. This was not something my father would usually say. This was not his language, and though I had always wanted him to speak differently, more correctly, I did not at all like the sound of those words in his mouth.

'Are you going to fight?' I asked again. 'Are you going to do something?'

He didn't answer my question. Instead, he only looked at me. 'Something's different about you,' he said. 'It's your arm. Your sling is gone. Look at that, Jenny.'

'Yeah,' she said.

I took my coat off then and looked down at myself, swinging my injured arm back and forth. It was skinnier, bonier than my other arm as a result of all those weeks just hanging at my side and doing nothing. 'I guess I'm better,' I said.

'Good for you,' he said.

'You fought over this,' I said, lifting my skinny arm up. 'You made sure things worked out.'

'Did I?' He looked down at his glass. I wished that he'd at least look at me. 'This is complicated, Steven. We might not get what we want this time.'

I understood then that something had already happened, that an agreement had already been reached, that my father had somehow already made the decision to stop fighting, that he had already quit. 'I slept too long,' I said. 'I shouldn't have slept so long. Someone should have woken me up. Why didn't anyone wake me up, Jenny?' She didn't say anything. 'Why is Jenny so quiet? What's wrong with Jenny?' I asked.

'I'm not so quiet,' she said.

'So tell me why nobody woke me up,' I said.

'I don't know,' she said, raising her voice. 'Stop asking me so much.'

'Why are they outside talking?' I asked my father.

'I'd guess they already have secrets to keep from us,' he said.

'What secrets?' He shrugged, though I had a feeling that he knew and didn't want to tell me. 'Where are Curtis Smith's kids?'

'They're at their aunt's house,' Jenny said.

'What secrets?' I asked again.

'Ask your mother,' my father said. It was the first time in our conversation that his voice had risen from resignation into anger. He looked out the giant window in front of us and said very quietly, 'A million-dollar view'.

The front door opened and closed, and we heard Curtis and my mother hang their coats up and stomp their feet and walk into the living room. Their faces were red from the cold outside. My mother was no longer wearing makeup, and her eyes were swollen. She'd been crying again. 'Why don't you sit down, Steven?' Curtis Smith said. I hadn't really noticed that I had been standing until he said that. So I sat down next to my father.

Curtis and my mother remained standing behind the couch opposite my father and me. My mother had neither looked at me nor said a word since she had entered the room, not so much as a 'Hi' or 'How are you?' or 'Did you sleep well?' She just stood there looking down at the carpet. I don't know how long my father and I sat in that very uncomfortable silence. 'I'm sitting down now,' I finally said. I wanted everybody to see that I was behaving, that I was done throwing tantrums. I thought that would help. I thought that might make a difference.

'Would you like more water?' Curtis asked my father.

My father looked at the remaining water in his glass. 'I think we should go ahead and get this over with,' he said.

'What's happening?' I asked. It was uncomfortable looking up at them. 'I wish everybody would sit down,' I said.

Curtis sat down next to Jenny, but my mother didn't. 'Why don't you sit down, Mary?' he asked her. She finally sat down, and as soon as she did, I noticed the aluminum finger cast on her right hand, which she'd kept behind her back until then. She laid that hand delicately in her lap and let it rest there. You could tell that it still hurt her.

'Oh,' I said. 'You went to the hospital?'

'Yes,' my mother said. She looked at me now. 'We did.'

'I did that?' I asked.

'Yes.'

'I'm sorry.'

'You're sorry?' Her voice wasn't exactly angry. It was baffled, confused. 'You swung a bat at me, Steven.'

'He said he was sorry,' my father said. I could tell that he wanted to protect me.

'I didn't mean to. I really didn't.' My mother looked down at her lap.

My father put a hand on my shoulder and nodded. 'We know that you didn't mean to,' he said.

I was beginning to understand what was happening to me, and I guess my father saw this in my face, since he looked away from me and out the window at the city below. 'Why's Noir here?' I asked. 'Why did Dad bring Noir? Is he going to live in this house, too?' Curtis Smith sat directly across from me, staring down at the glass top of the coffee table. It was obvious to me that nobody in the room would look in my direction.

'I thought you might like to say hi to him,' my father

said. 'I thought he might make things easier.'

'What things?' I asked again. 'Somebody please tell me.'

'Your father is here to take you home,' my mother finally said.

'Oh,' I said. My father and I looked at each other then. Despite his exhaustion, his paleness, the small, tender scabs on his cheek and chin from having shaved himself too closely, I saw clearly in his face what he wanted from me. I saw that he wanted me to be happy about what was about to happen. I saw that he needed me to be with him.

'Curtis and I have been talking,' she said. 'We think it might be best if you didn't stay here for now.'

'I have to leave?' I asked.

'You don't seem to want to stay here, Steven.'

'I said I was sorry.' I couldn't speak for a minute. 'What if I want to stay here?' I asked. 'Maybe I want to stay here. Maybe I do.'

'You don't, really,' my mother said. 'We don't think you do.'

'I want to stay,' I said. I couldn't stop myself from saying that.

'Listen to that,' my father finally said. He slapped his hands down in his lap. 'He wants to stay here, Mary.'

'No, I don't,' I said. But we all seemed to hear the falseness in my voice. 'Jenny is staying here?' I asked. 'Are you staying here?' I asked her.

Jenny didn't look up from her lap when she said, 'I guess. For a while.'

My father looked at my mother. 'This,' he said, 'is one

mess I didn't make. Don't you ever hold me responsible
for what is happening in this room right now.'

'Okay, Billy,' my mother said. She turned to me. 'It's
not just my decision. Other people are involved here.
Curtis doesn't know you yet. He thinks it might be best.
Just for now. He's worried about his kids. You scared
them yesterday. You even scared your sister.' She was
shaking her head now, and I guessed why Curtis's kids had
gone to the aunt's house. They would stay over there – at
a safe distance from me – until I had left. 'To tell you the
truth, you scared me. You really did, Steven.'

'I'm sorry,' I said. I faced Curtis Smith, who was still
too nervous and too much of a coward to look at me. He
was lightly drumming his fingers over the coffee table.
'You're letting him kick me out?'

'I'm sorry, too,' Curtis said, his voice very calm. 'We
don't know what else to do at this point.'

'I can't promise Curtis anything about what you will or
won't do next,' my mother said. 'I have no idea what to
expect from you myself.'

'First you want me to stay. Then you make me leave.'

'In a while,' she said, 'you can come back and we can
try this again, if you want.'

'A while? What does a while mean?'

'It will depend on you. It will be when you're ready.
When you're not so angry.'

'I'm not angry.'

'You were angry yesterday. You were out of control,
Steven.'

'I'll behave,' I said to her, trying not to raise my voice, trying to show her that I was in control. 'I'm behaving now. Aren't I behaving now?' She didn't say anything. I looked over at my father, who just sat there in his oversize suit staring at that stupid water glass in his hand. I hated seeing him like that. I hated knowing that she had been right the day before when she had called me my father's son. I hated knowing that she saw me as she saw him: We were too much trouble to love, too dangerous and unpractical to love because finally, as she had said, love didn't change anything. 'Do something,' I told my father. 'You need to do something. You have to.'

My father reached out and put his hand on my back. 'You need to calm down, Steven,' he said.

'I am calm,' I said. And I was calm. I was showing everyone that they could trust me, that I was done going crazy. 'Jenny's going to stay here?' I asked again. I was trying to imagine what living without my Bilmorette sister would be like. I was already somehow missing her, imagining the quiet in our house without her, the quiet that had been so unexpected to my father the night before.

'She says she wants to,' my mother said.

'When will we see each other?' I asked. Jenny just sat there, looking down at her lap.

'That will be worked out,' my mother said. She closed her eyes and then opened them again. 'This will all get easier later on. You'll see.' I couldn't tell what she was thinking or feeling, though I knew that she no more believed that things would become easier than I did. 'We went shopping today,' she said, gesturing at a cream-colored Nordstrom's bag beside the couch. 'I got you some new clothes.'

'Those aren't my clothes,' I said. I lifted the white garbage bag at my feet. 'These are my clothes.'

'You're going to freeze in this weather. You only have those terrible pajamas on.' I heard the sadness in her voice – too much sadness. 'You'll be able to come back soon. This will only be for a while.' It would not just be for a while, though, and I half knew it then; I half suspected then that I would stay with my father, that that would be my part in all of this. 'Okay?' she said.

'Okay,' I said, because I knew she wanted me to say that. Then we all just sat there in silence, and the calmness of that room bothered me. It wasn't right to sit quietly at a moment like that. Somebody needed to do something. That's all I could think. Somebody needed to act. We couldn't just say and do nothing. But we did, until my father finally looked up from his water glass and said, 'I think we need to go now.'

8

My father was too distracted that afternoon to ask for change when he handed the cab driver a fifty. I could guess where that money had come from, and half wanted the driver to have it. But I also knew we'd need every last dollar of it, so I demanded the change as soon as my father headed for the Buick. 'You're supposed to leave me a tip, kid,' the driver said. He looked like he might strangle me if I didn't, so I gave him the two dollars that I'd taken from the table at Dee's. 'That'll do,' he said, and drove away.

Noir was his usual unrestrained and happy self, and for the first time that I can remember, I hated him for it. When we let him out of the cab, he jumped on me and howled and yelped and wanted to play. His eyes were so goddamned joyful and he kept looking at me as if I were the same person he knew from the day before and the day before that, as if nothing at all had happened. I wanted those stupid, expectant eyes to stop looking at me. Inside the Buick, the air was freezing, and my father and I sat without talking. The blank white of the frozen windows surrounded us. For some reason, my father didn't get out and scrape. Instead, we sat there for what seemed like hours as the defroster slowly melted the ice away and revealed that huge, obscene house. When Noir refused to stay in the back of the Buick, and leapt into the front, where he too greedily begged for affection, I kicked him. 'Shut up!' I yelled, kicking him again.

'You kick him once more,' my father said, turning toward me, 'and I'll give you something you won't ever forget.'

My father had never cared much about Noir, who lunged again into the backseat where he lay on the floor, whimpering and hiding from me. 'He won't shut up,' I said.

'I brought him,' my father said, holding on to the steering wheel with both hands, 'to make this whole thing a little easier for you. That's why he's here. He's not here to be beat up by you.'

'It's not any easier,' I said.

'Don't kick him again. You got that?'

'Yes,' I said.

We pulled out of the driveway. The roads, which had frozen overnight, were dangerous. A few times as we made our way down the Avenues, the Buick seemed about to lunge off the asphalt. We fishtailed and once turned sideways – the whole car seeming about to careen into a tail spin. It felt as though we were traveling on air, as if the road had disappeared. But the car straightened out, and neither my father nor I was scared, a fact that seemed to keep the very real danger away. 'She'll come back to us,' he said. 'You'll see. She will.' But he said that without any enthusiasm, without any of his mindless, belligerent optimism, betraying the fact that he himself did not believe those words. I just sat there, next to my father, trying not to think and looking out at the blue sky and white sun, the bright afternoon that did not at all reflect the freezing temperatures that would fall into minus double digits later that night and somehow shatter the window of my bedroom so that, waking alone in the dark the next morning, I was cold, afraid, and unable to comprehend how the wind could be blowing through my room, scattering my school papers over the floor. I'd had a dream, and couldn't stop seeing the picture of that huge propeller from the Bone Yard being carted away through rows and rows of dismantled aircraft. 'This is where the planes come to die,' the air force guide, a blond man with a permanent smile on his face, kept telling my father and me. The guide wore aviator sunglasses with mirrored lenses behind which he seemed to hide some terrible knowledge. I tried to break through the confusion of that dream, of that sudden waking. I tried to understand where I could be and who I was and what had happened, until finally I saw that I was in bed at home, that my window had broken, and I was able to walk around the shattered glass and wake my father, who taped a garbage bag over my window and put me back in bed and said, even as the ravenously. The grape Kool-Aid made our mouths look bruised and swollen. I let Noir stay inside that night, and he lay under the table, shamelessly begging until I lowered a spoonful of mac and cheese, then another and another, and he licked greedily at the food, instantly forgiving me, instantly trusting me again.

'You smell a little,' my father said, looking at me funny. I lowered my head and smelled myself, realizing then that the dead man was at the table with us – the smell of him, anyway. My father didn't ask me to leave the table or wash. He was too exhausted to do anything more than make the comment, and I was too exhausted to let the smell bother me much. I had to think of Oak Groves, though, of Mrs. Smith and her crazy endless dinner that seemed to make her so insanely happy. I was sorry for ever having hurt her. She had just been living out a dream in a place where, without dreams, you would have died in a few minutes. That's all she'd done. And I wished then that my father and I had all those strange dishes, half of which I'd never eaten or even seen before – pumpkin soup, butternut squash, collard greens, grits and cheese, chutney, goose, partridge and pheasant, wild rice, and giblet gravy. I wished we'd had them if only as an excuse to talk to one another, to be polite, to say please pass this and that, to say thank you and you're welcome, and to say how delicious everything was in a genuine tone of voice that we hadn't even used a month before while eating so many foods for which we had no taste and ended up throwing out. But I couldn't imagine how expensive a dinner like that would be, and I remembered the large, empty round table at which old Mrs. Smith, gone in the head, sat asking for things that weren't there. At least the things we had on our table – the saucepan of mac and cheese, the Kool-Aid and mixed vegetables, the loaf of Wonder bread, the butter on a plate – were all real. I looked up at those things and said to my father, 'Please pass the bread and butter, if you wouldn't mind.'

He looked at me, a little confused. 'It's right in front of you,' he said. Our table was very small.

'Please pass the bread and butter,' I said again. He hesitated; then he did as I asked. 'Thank you,' I said. When he said nothing, I insisted, saying it a little louder, 'Thank you.'

'You're welcome, for God's sake,' he said. You could hear the anger in his voice. It wasn't anger at me. It was anger at everything. I knew it was that kind of anger because I felt it, too, anger and something like fear, and every word I said was alive with it. Nonetheless, I asked for the mixed vegetables, the mac and cheese, and the pitcher of Kool-Aid in the same polite way, and without looking at me he slowly reached for these things and put them down in front of me.

After a while, he looked up at me, his eyes dark, and said, 'Please pass the Kool-Aid,' and I did. 'Please pass the vegetables and the bread,' he said. And I did that, too. I did it, and then I looked at him and waited for what would come next.

Acknowledgments

Many thanks to Nicholas Delbanco and the New York Writers Institute's Master Writer Fellowship for providing money and mentorship during this novel's final stages. I would also like to thank friends who read this book and gave valuable advice:

Eric Gudas, Joshua Henkin, Chris Shainin, Porter Shreve, and Ian Reed Twiss. For their dedication and hard work, I am grateful to my agent, Alicka Pistek, and my editor, Joshua Kendall. I am also grateful to Ian Fulcher for sharing his expertise about all things Mormon; to my brother, Ben Fulton, for correcting my Salt Lake City geography; and to Dr. Paul Sorum for helping with medical details. I owe my family a debt of gratitude for their encouragement and faith. And finally, for her advice, generosity, and tireless support, Eve.